my so-called life

The Tragically Normal Diary of Rachel Riley

D0048051

my so-called life

The Tragically Normal Diary of Rachel Riley

by Joanna Nadin

OXFORD
UNIVERSITY PRESS

OXFORD
UNIVERSITY PRESS

Great Clarendon Street, Oxford OX2 6DP

Oxford University Press is a department of the University of Oxford.
It furthers the University's objective of excellence in research, scholarship,
and education by publishing worldwide in

Oxford New York

Auckland Cape Town Dar es Salaam Hong Kong Karachi
Kuala Lumpur Madrid Melbourne Mexico City Nairobi
New Delhi Shanghai Taipei Toronto

With offices in

Argentina Austria Brazil Chile Czech Republic France Greece
Guatemala Hungary Italy Japan Poland Portugal Singapore
South Korea Switzerland Thailand Turkey Ukraine Vietnam

Oxford is a registered trade mark of Oxford University Press
in the UK and in certain other countries

British Library Cataloguing in Publication Data
Data available

Printed in Great Britain

Paper used in the production of this book is a natural,
recyclable product made from wood grown in sustainable forests.
The manufacturing process conforms to the environmental
regulations of the country of origin.

december

Saturday 25

Christmas Day

Christmas presents asked for:

- mobile phone
- *O.C.* Complete First Season boxed set on DVD
- Chanel No. 5, as worn by Marilyn Monroe
- Touche Eclat to cover up hideous dark circles inherited from Granny Clegg
- hair straighteners to tame hideous curly hair inherited from Grandpa Clegg.

Presents received:

- Mum and Dad—BBC *Pride and Prejudice* boxed set. Apparently *The O.C.* has been added to Mum's list of proscribed items (also featuring *EastEnders* (common), *Coronation Street* (northern and common) and Ribena (purple, causing stain issues)). When I asked her why, she said it gave teenagers an unrealistic image of life in a seaside community. This is because she grew up in Cornwall where Granny Clegg made her wear a balaclava to school.
- James, my brother—*What Not to Wear* by Trinny and Susannah. This is rich coming from a seven year old who has been known to go out dressed in a Virgin Mary outfit.
- Grandpa Riley—a box of toffee with 'Thank you for looking after my dog' on it, which is weird as I have never looked after his dog because it *a*) is sick all the

time; *b*) looks at me menacingly; and *c*) ate one of my pink Converse low-rise. Maybe it is a plea. I hope not.

- Granny and Grandpa Clegg—a £5 WHSmith token and a Selection Box (sell-by date last August). The concept of inflation has clearly not reached St Slaughter yet, along with central heating and Channel 5.
- Auntie Joy(less) and Uncle John—a junior New Testament. They are severe Methodists and force my cousins to go to a cult church in Redruth where they dip you in a pool in all your clothes and talk in tongues.
- Uncle Jim—nothing. I don't think they celebrate Christmas in Tibet.
- Scarlet, my best friend—this diary.
- Sad Ed, practically next-door neighbour and second best friend—*The Bell Jar* by Sylvia Plath. Ed's ambition is to become an alcoholic genius and die in a car crash by the age of thirty. He has no chance. He passed out at Scarlet's birthday party after two martinis, can only play 'Bobby Shaftoe' on his guitar, and came third last in the school poetry competition last year.

Emailed Scarlet. She got: a Nokia with an inbuilt MP3 player, camera, and the *O.C.* theme as the ringtone; *The O.C.* Complete First Season boxed set; a Cure T-shirt and a pair of enormous skate trousers (she is thinking of

4

becoming either a goth or Avril Lavigne); and a book called *Let's Talk About Sex*. This is typical. Scarlet's mum is a sex therapist and her dad is a gynaecologist, which sounds exotic, but is, as Scarlet points out, actually gross. Especially when they start talking about pelvic floors at breakfast.

Casually mentioned Scarlet's new mobile phone to Mum. She said Scarlet would fry her brain with radiation. I said if I had one I would only use it to text people but Mum said I would get RSI and fail my GCSEs (which, I might add, are two years away). So now I am the only thirteen year old in Saffron Walden forced to use the public phone box to call Dad for a lift, which is embarrassing, not to mention unhygienic. I know for a fact that Mark Lambert once got his thing sucked in there by Leanne Jones for £2.50 and a Westlife CD.

Ate Bounty, Twirl, Mars bar, and half a Twix from out-of-date Selection Box whilst reading *What Not to Wear*. Apparently I am committing a litany of crimes against fashion. Under no circumstances should someone of my height (157 cm—only five cms off being a medical midget, according to James) wear cropped trousers. Looked in wardrobe to assess situation. Own three pairs cropped trousers, one pair of jeans (with a burn hole in the knee where James tried to invent inkstain remover), a bridesmaid's dress left over from Uncle Jim's second wedding, a kilt (don't ask), four assorted Marks & Spencer jumpers, a hoodie, seven T-shirts (three black,

5

one grey, one Brownies, one Saffron Walden Carnival, and one 'I Love Bodmin Farm Park'), and my school uniform. Not promising.

10 p.m.
Feel a bit sick. Maybe should have stopped at the Mars bar. Sylvia Plath would have stopped at half a Bounty. Or, probably, would have chosen an apple instead.

Sunday 26
Boxing Day
A terrible thing has happened. Grandpa Riley's dog has been banned from the Pink Geranium sheltered housing complex after eating the turkey for the communal Christmas lunch. Grandpa says it wasn't the dog, but, according to the warden, Mrs Peason, a pile of incriminating sick was found outside Elsie Stain's porch. Apparently it is the last straw in a long list of canine misdemeanours. She has asked Dad to come and pick it up this week or it will be sent to the dog home. That box of toffee must have been a premonition.

Also, a giant tidal wave has washed away Thailand. Mum says that's the problem with choosing the third world as a holiday destination—not only are the toilet arrangements suspicious but it is ravaged by freak weather, which is why Cornwall is ideal. James pointed out that Granny Clegg still had an outside toilet and

6

that it had rained persistently on three out of the last four visits to Cornwall, at which point he got sent to his room to reflect on world disaster.

Emailed Scarlet but no reply. She is obviously too busy watching *The O.C.* whilst wearing enormous skate trousers and reading about her G-spot. Went round to see Sad Ed. He was depressed, as usual. Mainly because he got a David Beckham calendar and a machine that dispenses miniature Dairy Milks for Christmas. He had asked for a stuffed crow and a box of Slimfast (he wants to get in shape for his tragic untimely death—he says he cannot be a revered genius with fat upper arms). He has not liked David Beckham since Year Five but his mum and dad are in denial. He said the Tsunami is a symbol of globalization and the capitalist society eating itself. I had to leave as he was making me depressed as well.

. . . .

Monday 27

Bank Holiday (UK)

Gave up waiting for email reply and went round to Scarlet's. Suzy and Bob (Scarlet gets to call her mum and dad by their first names) are frantically setting up a Tsunami appeal fund with the Saffron Walden Labour Party and Suzy's tantric yoga group. Scarlet was too busy to watch *The O.C.* as she was helping Suzy write letters to Sainsbury's and Tesco's demanding they hand over tinned oriental produce for immediate repatriation. Even

Scarlet's brother, Jack, is doing something. His band, Certain Death, are playing a charity gig at the Bernard Evans Youth Centre next week.

I tried calling my mum Janet once and she banned me from watching *Dawson's Creek* for two weeks.

Dad is going to fetch the dog tomorrow. Mum is not happy but has agreed, under a three strikes and it's out rule regarding food theft and vomiting.

Tuesday 28
Bank Holiday (UK)

Went to collect Grandpa's dog from the Pink Geranium sheltered housing complex, which sounds like an exotic gay nightclub but is a three-storey concrete block of flats on the site of the former gasworks. Mrs Peason the fascist warden was waiting at the front door with Grandpa and the dog, who looked very sad. (Grandpa, not the dog. The dog was eating a Mars bar and was too busy to look sad.) Mrs Peason said, 'At last. This dog is a menace to health and safety. I hope you have a ready supply of Jif.' Grandpa shook his head and said things like, 'It's all over for me and you now, pal. Don't pine yourself to death.' But the dog just climbed in the boot. I think it was glad to get away from Mrs Peason.

Mum has told Dad that the dog is not allowed into the lounge, dining room, or bedrooms, except in cases of absolute emergency (what would these be, I wonder?).

She has put up James's old stairgate on the kitchen door to restrict its activities.

8 p.m.
The dog has chewed through the stairgate and is locked in a stand-off situation in Mum and Dad's bedroom, where it is growling menacingly from under the sprig-patterned duvet cover.

Wednesday 29

Went into town with James and spent my £5 WHSmith token on *Sugar Rush* by Julie Burchill. Scarlet has read it twice and says it is seminal. James bought a dictionary of Elvish and a Carol Vorderman Sudoku puzzle book.

Rival Tsunami appeals are appearing all over the place. I counted at least five in the space of 500 yards, including one by Les Brewster and his wife, Ying, who own the Siam Smile Thai café on the High Street (formerly the Dog and Bucket pub). Les (overweight, bald, fifty-seven) divorced Mrs Brewster (also overweight, bald, and fifty-seven) two years ago and married Ying (thin, full head of hair, twenty-one) after a holiday in Phuket with the pub darts league. They are raising money to rebuild the sex bar where they met.

Got back to find that the dog had eaten the DVD player and the *Pride and Prejudice* boxed set. Dad claims it is not the dog but there is a pile of sick by the dog's bowl with a picture of Colin Firth in it. Mum says it is two strikes down but James says DVDs do not count as food.

Thursday 30

Tomorrow is New Year's Eve. I have still not been invited to any parties but I know that Jack is having all the members of Certain Death over for a jamming session and that will include Justin Statham (lead guitar) who can play the solos out of 'Stairway to Heaven' and 'I Believe in a Thing Called Love'. Scarlet says Jack says he is going out with Sophie Jacobs whose dad invented Microwave Muffins and who was once in a Fairy Liquid advert, but everyone knows she is still in love with Chris Cross (seriously), who is in quarantine for glandular fever, so as soon as he is given the all-clear it will all be over with Justin and I will be there to comfort him. I just need to lay some groundwork now. I will call Scarlet in the morning and get myself invited over.

Read three pages of *Sugar Rush*. Scarlet is right. It is clearly a modern classic. Why, oh why, can we not move to Brighton, which is full of exotic and tragic people like blacks, lesbians, and the homeless? All Saffron Walden has is Barry the Blade, the notorious town madman, who eats leftover falafel from the dustbin outside Abrakebabra. Where is the urban degradation? Where is the multicultural melting pot?

Friday 31

New Year's Eve

11.45 p.m.

New Year's Eve has been a total disaster. I should be at a house party having meaningful conversations on the stairs with Justin Statham but am, in fact, at home watching Jonathan Ross. Scarlet was too busy to celebrate—Suzy and Bob are holding a candlelit vigil with Les Brewster and Ying in the Siam Smile (they have joined forces in an attempt to form one giant Tsunami Appeal and weed out the pretenders). I asked if I could go but Mum said that the sex bar being washed away was probably a good thing and that anyway, she needed me to babysit so they can play Giant Jenga with Clive and Marjory next door. Sad Ed came over for a bit and we played his Leonard Cohen CD (he is a total Emotional Music Obsessive) but he has a 10 p.m. curfew. He says that we are both the products of depressingly unbroken homes and that is why our existence is so meaningless. Although his plight is worse than mine as his parents are both forty-eight, which makes them practically pensioners, and they are in the Aled Jones Fan Club.

Ed is right, I need more tragedy in my life. Why is life never like it is in books? Nothing Jacqueline Wilson ever happens to me: I am not adopted, my mum is not tattooed, I am not likely to move to the middle of a council estate or be put into care. My parents are not alcoholics, drug addicts, or closet transvestites. No one in

11

my family is brown, gay, interestingly autistic, or even mildly retarded (although James won't eat fruit and meat on the same plate and can sing the books of the Bible off by heart, which is a bit *Curious Dog*.) Even my name is pants. Why didn't my parents call me something exotic like Lola? (Actually I asked Mum that once and she said that no daughter of hers was being named after a transsexual prostitute.) In other words, my life is earth-shatteringly NORMAL.

This cannot go on. Something deep and life-changing has to happen. Thin Kylie (Britcher) was put into care for a week when her mum's breast implant burst. Even Fat Kylie (O'Grady) has suffered tragic loss—her dad Les choked to death on a Findus Crispy Pancake last March.

Next year will be different. It has to be. Starting tomorrow.

PEANUT →

COFFEE

PRIDE & PREJUDICE

january

Saturday 1

New Year's Day

8 a.m.

My New Year resolutions:

1. Drink coffee. Tragic heroines do not start the day with Cheerios and lemon barley.
2. Get boyfriend, i.e. Justin Statham.
3. Buy flattering clothes as suggested by Trinny and Susannah. Am not going to have a life-changing moment in a Brownies T-shirt and science experiment jeans. Am going to go vintage and look pale and interesting and incredibly literary.
4. Train dog. So far it has eaten, ripped up, or otherwise ruined: the DVD player, the *Pride and Prejudice* boxed set, a giant tin of Quality Street from Dad's work, two pairs of washing-up gloves, a bar of Clearasil soap, and a giant poster of Elijah Wood (James's, not mine. He is obsessed with him. His bedroom is a shrine to all things hobbit).
5. Get period. I am officially a freak of nature. I saw Fat Kylie's sister Paris-Marie buying Tampax in Boots three weeks ago and she is only 11.
6. Befriend more tragic and interesting people.
7. Visit Paris—centre of literary romance (e.g. *Sex and the City* final episode).

9.30 a.m.

New Year resolution amendment:

15

1. Drink tea. Tried making black coffee with Mum's Nescafé Gold Blend but felt a bit strange and had to lie down for half an hour. I think it is like drugs. You do not start off by injecting heroin. You need to try the softer stuff first. Tea is very vintage anyway. I bet Sienna Miller drinks tea.

2 p.m.
Tried training dog to no avail. It just wagged its tail when I told it to sit, then it lost interest and went off to chew some more of the kitchen wall.

Sunday 2

Took the dog to visit Grandpa Riley. Grandpa's care worker Treena was there, smoking a Benson and Hedges. James pointed out that forty-nine per cent of smokers die from lung or heart disease and that, anyway, Mrs Peason had banned smoking in the flats after Grandpa accidentally set fire to himself when he fell asleep during *Cocoon*. Treena muttered, 'Flaming weirdo,' and opened the window. She is not very caring for a care worker.

The dog seemed happy to see Grandpa and Grandpa got all teary like it was Lassie coming back home but then it ate Treena's cigarettes and was sick on the rug. Treena said, 'They cost me £5.15 they did.' So Grandpa gave her ten pounds, which made her a whole lot more caring. She gave Grandpa a kiss and offered to 'do his feet' later. Vile. I have seen Grandpa Riley's feet. They are huge and the toenails are yellow.

Monday 3
Bank Holiday (UK)

Auntie Joyless and Uncle John were supposed to be coming to stay this week but she rang to say they couldn't as they were having discipline issues with Boaz (who is also thirteen, but three months younger than me in actual time and about three years in mental time). Apparently he is refusing to go to Bible camp this Easter. Anyway it is a relief as Auntie Joyless would be bound to ask me if I was reading the New Testament and I would have to tell the truth (she has a spooky sixth sense about lying) and say I was reading *Sugar Rush*, which is about lesbians and sex, and then she would make Mum ban it, like she did with Boaz's *Harry Potter*.

The dog and James are best friends. He speaks to it in Elvish, which seems to calm it down. It will not leave his side and follows him when he goes to the toilet, guarding the door like Cerberus at the gates of hell. He has trained it using biscuits (it gets a digestive for sitting, and a custard cream for lying down. James is thinking of patenting the method).

Tuesday 4

Bank Holiday (Scotland)

Mum has banned the biscuit method. She says she is not forking out £2.33 a day on dog treats. (The dog ate two packets each of digestives and custard creams plus four Duchy Originals chocolate ginger things that only come out when we have guests.)

Wednesday 5

Two days to go until Jack's gig. My clothing options are: grey T-shirt, hoodie, and kilt or outlawed cropped trousers. Looked in Mum's wardrobe for possible vintage outfits. Could only find a hideous mint-green jumpsuit with criminally tapered legs left over from the eighties. I have to go shopping.

4 p.m.

There is a distinct lack of vintage clothing in Saffron Walden unless you count Gray Palmer, which only sells Aertex and tweed. Went to Oxfam in the hope of unearthing a beaded flapper dress or ethnic-print kaftan. Mrs Simpson was in there. She smells of wee and wears white flares all year round, which is not a good colour when your hygiene is questionable.

There was no flapper dress or kaftan. Bought an enormous jumper, a crochet top, a suede miniskirt, and some furry boots. Mrs Simpson bought a pair of tap shoes and a Wonderbra. Maybe she is auditioning for the Amateur Operatic Society's production of *Chicago* (starring forty-seven-year-old Co-op cashier Maureen Tyler as Renée Zellweger).

Wore my giant jumper. James said I looked and smelt like the dog and Dad asked if I wanted to go for a walk (ha ha).

8 p.m.
I have three bites on my stomach. That dog has got to be defleaed.

. . . .

Thursday 6
Epiphany
What is epiphany?

Went round to Sad Ed's to show him my new vintage look. He agrees it is more tragic and literary than my old style. He is not coming to the gig as he has to go to his cousins' in Leighton Buzzard. He says he doesn't care because Certain Death are just amateurs and he is getting tickets to see Pete Doherty at a secret Babyshambles gig in London. (In his dreams. The last concert he was allowed to go to was the Teletubbies live at Harlow Playhouse.) He is just jealous because he once auditioned to play lead guitar but they picked Justin because his dad's company has got a Transit van. Also, Justin is quite good and Ed is truly crap.

19

Two more bites, including one on my neck. I am going to be disfigured at this rate. I hope it is dark at the gig. Justin is not going to want to cry on a spotty shoulder.

Friday 7

6 p.m.

Am wearing crochet top, suede skirt, and furry boots. Scarlet is wearing her Cure T-shirt and giant skate trousers. She says she is hovering more towards goth but that Suzy won't let her dye her hair black so she needs a back-up in case the other goths reject her. Suzy said my vintage outfit was 'fabulous' and said she would look out some old Monsoon skirts for me. Jack said 'Interesting boots, Riley,' but I couldn't tell if he was being sarcastic or not because his hair is so long it covers most of his face. He got sent home from school once to get a haircut, but Suzy set up a protest group and the headmaster, Mr Wilmott, was forced to retract the suspension for fear of mass hair growing. Am staying at Scarlet's tonight, which means I get to stay and help the band pack up. I am almost a groupie.

10 p.m. Scarlet's bedroom

The gig was a disaster. Sophie Jacobs and her minions Fi and Pippa were there. They were all wearing pink in unironic homage to *Mean Girls*, which they have seen thirty-seven times. Sophie was draped over Justin looking all blonde and ethereal (Chris Cross is still bed-ridden). She asked me why I was wearing her gran's boots. I told her they were vintage but she said, 'No they're not, they're Clarks, my mum took them to Oxfam last week.' Then she and Justin laughed and they walked off together to the VIP area (aka the parent and toddler room).

Scarlet is still in the bathroom being sick. She got the goths to buy her two rum and blacks. Then she tried to stage dive but no one caught her and she hit Sophie Jacobs and passed out. Her dad had to take us home before Certain Death had even got on stage. She threw up in the map pocket on the back of her dad's seat on the way, but I don't think he noticed as he had Coldplay ('middle-class semi-talented bandwagon-jumping sellouts' according to Sad Ed) on very loud. At least Sophie has a black eye, so something good happened, anyway.

Saturday 8

Scarlet didn't come down for breakfast so I ate croissants with Bob, Suzy, and Jack. They were discussing literature so I said I was reading *Sugar Rush*. Bob said Julie Burchill is a man-hater with a voice like she's breathed in too much helium. Suzy narrowed her already cat-like eyes and said that Bob was only saying that because Julie Burchill used to be married to Bob's hero Tony Parsons but dumped him because he was a misogynist with a fake cockney accent. Jack said 'Whatever' and rolled his eyes at me. Why don't we have heated debates like this at home (or croissants, for that matter)? The closest we get is when Mum and Dad argue over who should be Round Table chairman now that Tony London has defected to Lions Club, and whether we have to visit Granny and Grandpa Clegg this year and, if so, do we take the M4 or A303?

Bob gave me a lift home. He asked if I could smell something funny but I diverted the question by pointing out some new graffiti on the bus shelter.

Sunday 9

1 p.m.
Scarlet is not allowed over. Her dad has found the Volvo sick. The rum and black has stained the beige leather indelibly.

The dog is in the shed and is refusing to come out. Mum tried to deflea it, which sent it into a wild panic and it made a bolt for freedom. It has changed colour from muddy grey to white, with all the powder. James is in the shed with it, talking Elvish to try and soothe it.

3 p.m.
The dog and James are out. They were won over with a packet of bourbons. They would be useless in a hunger strike.

5 p.m.
I have six more bites. The powder has not worked. Mum is taking the dog to the vet's next week while we are at school.

Monday 10
School. Tried to wear my enormous jumper over my uniform but Mum said it was called uniform for a reason. She does not understand vintage. She buys all her clothes from Marks & Spencer in the sale. How will Justin notice me now?

Registration was awash with Christmas iPods and mobile phones. Fat Kylie's Samsung plays a video of her little brother Brady (O'Grady, seriously) shouting, 'I don't want f**king Fruit Shoot, I want Cheese Strings.' He has a wide command of swear words for a three year old. Thin Kylie is not back from Lanzarote yet. Scarlet suggested Ms Hopwood-White report Mrs Britcher to social services, but Ms Hopwood-White is scared of the Kylies' mothers ever since parents' evening when she suggested they might like to stop smoking on school premises. We are getting someone new in our class called Davey MacDonald. He is being transferred from Mrs Duddy's Special Educational Needs group (aka Retards and Criminals). Maybe he will be an idiot savant like in that film with Tom Cruise and Dustin Hoffman. He will be tragically misunderstood but will go on to win the Nobel Prize. I shall befriend him.

Tuesday 11

Davey MacDonald is not an idiot savant. He is just an idiot who has a habit of getting his thing out in class. He was back with Mrs Duddy by 11 o'clock after he showed it to Scarlet in the language lab and asked her to help him with his 'special needs'. Ms Hopwood-White said he wasn't ready to be integrated yet. She told Scarlet to see the school counsellor (and woodwork teacher) Mr Doddington (aka Doddy) for trauma. Scarlet said she wasn't traumatized and that it looked bent and that he could suffer sexual problems later in life. She should know, she has seen hundreds in her mum's manuals at home. I haven't seen any. Except James's when Mum made us share a bath in one of her economy drives. I don't think that counts. I hope not.

The dog does not have fleas. Mr Mercer the vet says they must be from another source. He also said the dog has to stop eating so much, apparently it is showing signs of obesity, sugar addiction, and canine tooth decay.

Wednesday 12

Thin Kylie is back from Lanzarote. She is the colour of a Footballer's Wife. Sad Ed said he hoped it was from a bottle or she will be riddled with life-threatening moles by Year Twelve, but Kylie said, 'No, it's f**king real, you fat poof. I spent six hours a day on this.' She and Mark Lambert were all over each other in break. They have been going out six weeks. She has got a badge on her

Burberry parka from him for every time she has let him touch her minky. Which makes ten (five McFly, three Busted, one Girls Aloud, and one 'I've seen the lions of Longleat!'—I counted them in food technology). I heard her tell Mark she nearly died being parted from him. But later she showed Fat Kylie and Tracey Hughes pictures of a waiter called Jose.

The dog is sulking. Mum is forcing it to eat dry dog biscuits. It is used to three cans of Pal and several Penguins a day. It lies in front of the fridge, eyeing it mournfully. Mum says the dog will cave in before she does.

Thursday 13

I have four more bites. Where are these things coming from? Maybe there is a dead animal in the house. Clive and Marjory next door once found a dead squirrel under the drinks cabinet. Apparently it had got in through the window after seeing a packet of cashews. It still had the empty packet in its claws. Mum did a thorough sweep of the house after that and put locks on all the windows. I don't think the squirrels will be breaking in to get at her mung bean cultivator.

Friday 14

Oh my God. The source of the fleas has been identified. It is the enormous fluffy Oxfam jumper. Mum tried to handwash it and the fleas all jumped out of the sink and scattered around the kitchen. Rentokil have been round and fumigated the place. Mum made them park round the corner and take off their badges so that Marjory won't think her domestic hygiene has lapsed. Going vintage is fraught with difficulties.

Saturday 15

Went to see Grandpa Riley. The dog was not allowed to come after last time's cigarette fiasco. Grandpa and Treena were on the sofa watching T4. She was sitting very close to him. Clearly smoking has compromised her sense of smell or she would have kept away from the overpowering odour of Old Spice and athlete's foot powder. Grandpa says he is applying for a home visit next Sunday. I said I thought you only had to do that if you were in prison but Grandpa said Mrs Peason used to work at HMP Holloway and is implementing a strict new regime.

Sunday 16

The dog is victorious. Mum left it alone in the kitchen while she was on the phone to Granny Clegg (topics discussed: 'Why in God's name have Persil changed the smell of their washing powder?' and 'the impending downfall of St Slaughter now that Hester Trelowarren has turned one of her battery chicken sheds into a holiday home') and it managed to eat the entire, uncooked, Sunday lunch. Dad says it is Mum's fault for depriving it of real meat. It is back on Pal. Mum says she cannot afford to lose £10 worth of Waitrose organic lamb every week.

Monday 17

A life-changing moment has occurred, without the aid of vintage clothing: Justin Statham spoke to me. To be fair, I was behind him in the queue for the Coke machine and his exact words were, 'Got two fifties for a pound?' But Scarlet and I think it is a breakthrough, none the less. Sophie still has a black eye. If it lasts much longer he will chuck her for sure. She looks like a panda in a wig.

Tuesday 18

Scarlet and I lurked by the Coke machine all break and lunchtime in case Justin needed any 50ps but there was no sign of him. He must be getting his refreshment from other sources. Sad Ed says I am delusional, but how would he know? He has only ever been in love with Willow off *Buffy*, and she was a lesbian.

Grandpa Riley rang. Mrs Peason is allowing him out for four hours on Sunday. He has asked if he can bring a guest. I hope it is not his neighbour Arthur Edge. He has

27

a colostomy bag and Parkinson's, which is potentially very messy.

. . . .

Wednesday 19

Scarlet has tracked Justin down to Mr Patel's opposite the lower school gates. He goes there with Jack at lunchtime. Under interrogation from Scarlet, Jack has disclosed that he buys a Coke (full fat) and a Snickers. I am going to start eating Snickers to bond with him. I hope I am not allergic to peanuts. Ooh, if I was, though, he could heroically give me mouth to mouth when I collapse on Mr Patel's sticky lino.

. . . .

Thursday 20

Went to Mr Patel's at lunch and bought a Snickers, right in front of Justin and Sophie. But it turns out I am not allergic to peanuts. For a minute I thought I might be because I went all red and started coughing, but it turned out that a peanut had lodged in my throat. Sad Ed hit me on the back and the peanut flew out onto Sophie Jacobs's pink puffa. Sophie said, 'Gross, you loser'; Justin flicked the peanut on the floor for Sophie; Jack smiled and said, 'Nice one, Riley'; and I stood there with Snickers dribble running down my chin. It was not the bonding moment I had hoped for.

. . . .

Friday 21

I am avoiding Mr Patel's and peanut-based products for a while. Scarlet agrees I need to lie low at least until Sophie's coat is dry-cleaned. At the moment the peanut residue is still very much in evidence.

Saturday 22

A life-size cut-out of Des Lynam and a Will Young doll arrived today addressed to James. Mum has now added eBay to her banned list. She is writing to ask them to review their security arrangements, which are clearly insufficient if a seven year old can evade them. She has also asked Grandpa Riley to review his own security arrangements, as apparently he let James use his Mastercard after the sellers refused to accept £17.23 in small change and a Boots token. Dad just said, 'That boy is not normal, Janet.'

Sunday 23

Grandpa Riley's guest was not Arthur Edge; it was Treena. Mum went very tight-lipped when she saw her. She does not approve of Treena, who is not only northern, but watches *EastEnders*, smokes, and wears mauve leggings (even I would ban these). They brought a four-pack of Red Bull and a box of Ferrero Rocher with them. Mum asked Treena where her husband was and she said he was busy working for the post office. This is not strictly true. Grandpa told me later he is in prison but sews mailbags. So it is not a total lie either.

Lunch was a disaster. The dog got overexcited about the Ferrero Rocher and knocked over Treena's Red Bull in its frenzy to get at the table. Red Bull has been added to the proscribed list on account of its persistent stickiness.

Monday 24

I have chosen my GCSEs. I am doing the same as Scarlet and Sad Ed. Except for art, which I have been actively encouraged not to choose by Head of Art Beardy Morris, and music, which would be pointless as I can only play 'Twinkle Twinkle Little Star' on the descant recorder. I am doing: English literature (of course), English language, maths, French, biology, history, geography, drama, and rural studies (Jack says it is a cinch—all you have to do to pass is clean out the school chickens and grow some potatoes).

Tuesday 25

Robert Burn's birthday

There is an apostrophe in the wrong place in Robert Burns. Mum says it is symptomatic of the decline in educational standards under New Labour (she voted Lib

Dem). She is writing to Lynne Truss and WHSmith to inform them of the error.

Wednesday 26

There is uproar at school. Mr Patel's shop was burgled last night and is closed for police investigation, and the Coke and crisp machine is out of everything except plain chocolate Bountys and Polos. Lessons were disastrous on account of the sugar and caffeine withdrawal. Mr Wilmott has been forced to demand an emergency machine restocking.

Mr Patel is hoping CCTV footage will identify the thieves. Apparently they stole £12.37 from the charity jar (the sex bar Tsunami appeal), six cartons of Marlboro (high tar), four bottles of cherry brandy, and a jumbo box of Wotsits.

Thursday 27

The robbery has been solved. According to Tracey Hughes, whose mum is the receptionist at the police station, the CCTV wasn't working but they still know it was Stacey O'Grady (another of Fat Kylie's many brothers) and Darryl Stamp who works at B&Q. Darryl dropped his balaclava at the scene, which still had his name sewn in it from primary school. He buckled under interrogation and named Stacey as the ringleader. I wouldn't want to be in Darryl's shoes. Stacey once broke Fat Kylie's nose when she grassed him to her mum for stealing her fake Chanel handbag and Tiffany heart necklace and selling them to Darryl so he could give them to his mum for Christmas.

Friday 28

Mrs Hughes has been suspended from receptionist duties for disclosing police information. Tracey says she is only allowed to make tea and feed the police dogs for a month.

Saturday 29

The O.C. Season Two begins on Channel 4 tomorrow. My life will be complete once more. Although I will have to view it at Scarlet's every week as Mum is refusing to remove it from her banned list despite my pointing out that one of the lead characters is called Seth, which is Grandpa Clegg's middle name, i.e. as backward Cornish as you can get.

Sunday 30

Went to Scarlet's for the second annual *O.C.* opening episode ceremony. Suzy watched it as well. She is addicted to teen television. She was inconsolable when

Joey picked Pacey over Dawson. Even though Dawson's forehead was unfeasibly large. *The O.C.* was excellent and inspiring. Life would be so much better if I lived in California and had an ex-criminal living in my pool house or an ex-porn star for a mother.

Monday 31
Mum has written to the paper to complain about the increasing quantity of dog mess on Battleditch Lane (aka Dogshit Alley). She stepped in no less than three piles of poo on the way to St Regina's C of E primary today. She says if she can stoop to clear up after the dog, then so can everyone else. This means I will have the dog-owning mafia on my back at school come Friday once the paper is out. My week is doomed.

february

Gloss

← FURRY
VINTAGE
BOOT

← PANCAKE

SNOG
BADGE

Tuesday 1

Scarlet says the paper will call her mum and dad about the dog poo for a comment (they are both Labour councillors). I told her to tell them not to say anything but Scarlet says it is anti-social behaviour as well as environmental damage so they will probably demand a crackdown and on-the-spot fines.

Wednesday 2

I phoned the newspaper to try to recall the letter but the woman at the other end said the paper was going to print and the only changes from now on were tonight's lottery numbers. I asked her what would happen if a serious front-page crime were committed right now. She said it would appear on page seven next week. I told her the *Guardian* did not get where it is with this lax attitude to breaking news. She said she wouldn't know, she only read Mystic Meg.

The paper does not get delivered until after school tomorrow, so I will only have Friday to suffer. I have to be grateful for small mercies.

Thursday 3

Mum's dog poo letter has made the second page of the *Walden Chronicle* under the headline 'Dog Mess Mania', alongside a photo of some poo, possibly on Battleditch Lane, but feasibly anywhere.

The letter said:

DOG MESS MANIA

The state of Battleditch Lane, popular with parents for walking their children to school

(and with the Kylies for snogging during the lunch break)

is a disgrace to the town. It is high time that the council took the menace of dog mess seriously. It can cause blindness, stomach upset, not to mention the damage to footwear. The council must be urged to provide extra pooper scooper bins and to patrol the area day and night for lawbreakers.

Under the letter was a comment from Suzy. She says it is all the fault of the Tory council and has demanded that Hugo Thorndyke MP (Con.) lobby parliament for a dog poo crackdown and on-the-spot fines.

Under her comment was a comment from Hugo Thorndyke MP (Con.) who said it is all the fault of the Labour government for allowing anti-social behaviour to run riot in market towns.

This is humiliation beyond anything I have ever known. This is worse than when I had to partner Peter Foster (aka Stinky Pete) in country dancing at primary school, only an hour after he'd wet himself (again). Not even Scarlet would touch my hand for ages. I had to disinfect it with Dettol.

I cannot go to school tomorrow. This calls for desperate measures.

. . . .

Friday 4

My ploy of claiming a stomach bug failed, despite using Scarlet's tried and tested method of throwing a glass of water down the toilet whilst retching to make it sound like you are really being sick. Mum said there were no telltale vomit splashes on the toilet surround so she wasn't falling for that one. The police should employ her in forensics, she is like Amanda Burton.

School was predictable. Fat Kylie (whose dog, Tupac, is responsible for at least half the mess) said, 'They got to go somewhere, innit.' When I suggested she could just pick it up she said, 'I ain't touching no stinking dogshit, loser.' And Tracey Hughes said her mum said the police have got better things to do with their time than patrol for dog poo. I have seen the police dogs pooing down there as well so it is fair to say that would be pointless.

I told Mum what trauma her campaign was causing me but she said their reactions were typical of today's irresponsible dog-owners and that they should bring back the dog licence and raise it to £100. She is going to suggest it to the Lib Dems for their next manifesto.

Thank God it is Friday.

- -

Saturday 5

Scarlet and Sad Ed agreed I need to keep a low profile in Saffron Walden so we got her dad to drive us to the cinema in Cambridge. (Our cinema shut down in 1984 and is now a branch of Halfords.) Scarlet's dad's Volvo still smells, despite three Feu Orange air fresheners. But when we got to the cinema the man with the ginger toupee who runs the Odeon wouldn't let me see any vaguely interesting films as he said I didn't look twelve and would therefore need parental guidance. I told him I was nearly fourteen (in August) but he said he had never seen a thirteen year old with so little make-up and so many clothes (I was wearing one of Suzy's Monsoon dresses and the boots). Scarlet and Ed were allowed in as they both had eyeliner on. The only film the toupee man would sell me a ticket for was *Spongebob Squarepants* so I had to watch that with a cinema full of eight year olds full of nachos and pick-and-mix. I do not think it should have such a low certificate, it is full of sexual innuendo—he lives in Bikini Bottom, for goodness' sake—plus it is clearly drug-influenced, involving a pineapple under the sea. I left before the end after a Magnum stick got

40

entangled in my hair and went next door to Boots to buy some 17 make-up. Got supercurl mascara, a lipgloss called 'Juicy Lucy', and a green eyeshadow, which the assistant claimed would go with my hair, but which looks suspiciously like three-day-old bruising.

. . . .

Sunday 6

Wore green eyeshadow to breakfast. Dad asked if I had been in a fight (ha ha). James said, 'Don't think you're going out looking like that,' and Mum just tightened her lips. What chance do I stand against this kind of opposition?

Took the dog for a walk to the Pink Geranium sheltered housing complex so Grandpa could talk to it through the fence. The dog wasn't very interested, it is still recovering from its starvation diet, and it was too cold for Grandpa's bunions so there was not the emotional reunion I had hoped for. Grandpa asked if I had been bullied at school. Came home and removed green eye shadow. Will stick to mascara and subtle lipgloss, as worn by natural beauty Sienna Miller. Eyeshadow will be emergency cinema make-up only.

. . . .

Monday 7

Grandpa Clegg rang after school to moan about the hunting ban. He wants Mum to pass on his outrage to

Suzy in the hope she will tell Tony Blair. (Suzy met him once at a Gala dinner at the Chelmsford Moat House. Scarlet says she had to take a valium afterwards to calm down.) I don't know why Grandpa is up in arms, he has never been on a hunt in his life. The closest he gets is the Fox and Hounds in Camborne. He and Granny Clegg are joining the Countryside Alliance. I do not see them fitting in with the 4×4 set. They live in a 1950s terrace called 'Bellevue' (overlooking Hester Trelowarren's battery chicken farm) and think that the Harvester in Bodmin is posh.

He says they are thinking of going on the pro-hunting march in London on Saturday. Mum urged him not to. This is because it will involve them taking the train, and they got lost the last time they went to Plymouth and called 999 from a payphone. The policeman who took them back to the station told them not to leave the Redruth area in the near future except under strict supervision. Also, Grandpa Clegg is notoriously racist so Mum is worried he may say something untoward on the underground and get mugged or happy slapped.

- -

Tuesday 8
Shrove Tuesday

Ate compulsory pancakes. The dog got worked up with all the tossing and singed itself on the gas trying to intercept a pancake in mid-air. It looks weird. I am not walking it until the hair has grown back.

. . . .

Wednesday 9
Ash Wednesday
Have decided not to give anything up for Lent. The list of proscribed items in our house is now so lengthy that I don't think I need to deny myself anything as Mum is already doing it for me.

Sad Ed is giving up watching *Buffy* reruns. He will not last. He has no stamina when it comes to Willow in a lesbian clinch.

. . . .

Thursday 10
Islamic New Year
Ms Hopwood-White caused a stir by wishing Happy New Year to Ali Hassan, our Iraqi refugee. The Hassans are Church of England. Ali said she had insulted his religion and demanded an apology. Then Jade McDonald, whose mum is a quarter Jewish, asked her why they hadn't celebrated Hanukkah, and said that Ms Hopwood-White was clearly racist. Then Fat Kylie demanded Catholic concessions like Filet O'Fish on a Friday. Mr Wilmott had to be called in to calm everyone down. He said he was minded to instigate a no-religious-celebrations rule at school but then Sad Ed pointed out that he would have

to cancel Year Seven's production of *Jesus Christ Superstar* so he is having a temporary suspension until people can be sensible.

Friday 11

Mum has rung Grandpa Clegg again to plead with him to reconsider the hunting march. Grandpa Clegg says it is all arranged. Auntie Joyless is picking him and Granny up at 8 a.m. to take them to Truro. They are going to get the direct train to Paddington and will then follow the crowds to Hyde Park. Mum said she doubted there would be hordes of huntsmen walking through West London but Grandpa said, 'Well, if the feeling in St Slaughter is anything to go by, I think you will surprised, Janet. We are right livid in Cornwall. That Mr Blair is going to ride roughshod over our rural history and sell our souls to Brussels.' (Grandpa reads the *Daily Mail* religiously.) Mum pointed out that it was Margaret Thatcher who signed us up to the Common Market but then Grandpa Clegg put the phone down as he won't hear anyone speak ill of Mrs Thatcher.

Saturday 12

Granny and Grandpa Clegg did not make it to London. Apparently Auntie Joyless got her Mini Metro stuck behind a herd of 'new-fangled' organic sheep and the trip was aborted in favour of a shopping trip to Trago Mills. Grandpa says he got a seven-pack of pants for £3.99 and a jumbo box of Christmas crackers for £2.50.

. . . .

Sunday 13

Tomorrow is Valentine's Day. I fear the worst. Last year Scarlet and I got no cards. The Kylies got seven each. Scarlet says it is because they are so liberal with their sexual favours.

. . . .

Monday 14
St Valentine's Day

Not a single Valentine card. It is the school's fault for scheduling half-term to clash with this crucial occasion. If I was at school, someone could have put one on my locker. James got three. He is strangely popular for a nerd.

Rang Scarlet. She got a card but it is from Davey MacDonald in special needs—the idiot signed it. Scarlet says Valentine's Day is meaningless capitalist nonsense perpetuated by Clinton's Cards and Cadbury's in order to boost sales in the Christmas to Easter lull. She has put her card in the recycling bin.

Scarlet is right. I do not care about not getting a card, not even one from an exhibitionist retard. I am far too literary and interesting for such commercialism.

45

Read some more *Sugar Rush*. Maybe I should try lesbianism. I could be like Madonna when she kissed Britney, or the ginger one off *Sex and the City*.

3 p.m.
Tried thinking about naked women, but the only minky I have seen close up belongs to Thin Kylie who charged 50p to look at hers behind the mobile science labs last summer (I did not pay, I stumbled across it on my way to feed the locusts). I just kept hearing her voice saying, 'Piss off, Brian, it's one pound to touch it.' Anyway, she is definitely not gay and has the badges to prove it. The only possible lesbians at our school are the PE teachers Miss Beadle and Miss Vicar, who live together, and Oona Rickets in Year Ten who is a feminist and won't wear deodorant because it is masking woman's true nature. Mr Wilmott was forced to intervene during a heatwave last year. I hope I am not a lesbian. I do not want to have to kiss Oona Rickets.

4 p.m.
My lesbian phase is over. A valentine card has arrived, posted by hand! I interrogated James as to who had delivered it but he says he was too busy phoning his admirers. The card is of Millais's painting of Ophelia drowning after she goes mad because she is socially inferior to Hamlet etc. Inside it just has a question mark and a sticky stain, possibly a lover's tears, although it

46

smells like caramel. The £2.20 price sticker from Mr Patel's is still on the back, so it must have come from someone at school i.e. Justin! Justin is secretly in love with me! I am his Ophelia. Rang Scarlet and she says Jack says that he and Justin are doing *Hamlet* for GCSE, plus I am totally socially inferior to him! Scarlet agrees that, as the card came from Mr Patel's, it is helping keep corner shops alive against the omnipresent out-of-town supermarket giants (or Waitrose in our case), so it is OK to keep it.

I have pinned the card to my notice board.

Tuesday 15

Could not sleep for thinking about my card. If only I were a Shakespearean heroine. Life would be so much more interesting if my father was fatally stabbed by a tormented Justin in a case of mistaken identity, and then I went mad and drowned in a brook (i.e. the shopping-trolley-clogged Slade behind the police station), although I cannot see James piercing Justin with a poisoned rapier.

Decided to become more like Ophelia so I lay on the bed with my eyes shut in what I imagined was a sort of deathlike calm. But my hoodie and John Lewis duvet set didn't feel very Shakespearean so I put on my bridesmaid's dress and scattered some leaves and a bit of potting compost in the bath. It was a bit weird wearing clothes in the water at first because air came out from the bodice and made noises, but then I imagined Justin mourning my innocent body and got quite into it. The moment was ruined when Mum came in for an emergency wee (the downstairs loo has been blocked since Grandpa Riley's last home visit) and screamed blue murder. I assumed she thought I had committed suicide but apparently it was panic at the compost. She made me Cillit Bang the bath immediately. If I had slashed my wrists she would have got out her Stain Devils collection before calling an ambulance.

Sad Ed came over to see if I'd got any cards. I showed him the Ophelia one. He agreed that whoever sent it must be sensitive and meaningful. I said it was Justin and he said that that was impossible as Justin likes The Darkness who are pseudo-musicians. He is just sulking as he only got a card off his mum and dad, again.

. . . .

Wednesday 16

Went round Scarlet's. Apparently Suzy and Bob are not speaking to each other. It is all after last night's emergency Labour Party meeting. Both of them want to stand in the next election and cannot agree as to who will best represent a forward-thinking Saffron Walden. Bob says Suzy, being *a*) female and *b*) a sex therapist, will put off the crucial pensioner vote. Suzy says pensioners will not vote for an abortionist who likes Tony Parsons and

smoked cannabis until he was thirty-eight (i.e. last year).
Scarlet says the whole thing is hypothetical anyway as
neither of them have a hope of beating Hugo Thorndyke
MP (Con.) as he has a majority of 21,000, and the town
only has 22,000 people in it.

I was hoping Jack would be there so we could get
more information about my card but he was at band
practice at the Air-Training Corps hut (a youth group for
the criminally weapons-obsessed) so we went upstairs
and listened to Sad Ed's new vintage Smiths CD instead.
It was about being run over by double-decker buses,
which was all a bit depressing, so I went home to look at
my card again but the dog had got into my room and
smelt the caramel and now Ophelia's head is a bit chewed
and wet so she looks more like Jocelyn Wildenstein.
Nothing is sacred in this house.

Thursday 17

Went to town with Scarlet to lurk outside Goddard's
Butchers. Justin has a holiday job there mopping up
meat blood and operating the mincing machine. Was
hoping for some words of confirmation that he is my
Hamlet, but Sophie was in there with her mum buying
fillet steak and swishing her bottom-length blonde hair
everywhere (which is unhygienic in a butcher's—no
one wants Herbal Essences in their pork belly). Justin is
obviously having to keep up a pretence with Sophie to

spare her the devastating truth. She is notoriously highly-strung. She once tried to kill herself with a bottle of Junior Vitamin C tablets after she failed an audition for _Grange Hill_. Bought a scotch egg so as not to give the game away. I will bide my time. My day will come. Gave scotch egg to dog. It has been sick on video of _Heartbeat_.

Friday 18

Hunting has been banned from the British countryside (except for drag hunting, hare coursing, and if the fox dies before the hounds get to it and shred it to pieces). Went round Scarlet's as Suzy and Bob were having a party to celebrate this historic occasion. They say it is all about the miners, really. I am not sure what they mean. I did not think miners went hunting, unless they are talking about pit ponies. They have resolved the election issue. Suzy is going to stand and Bob is going to be her Chief of Staff if she gets in. Scarlet says that it was settled because the hospital said they couldn't give Bob time off in March and April due to the seasonal rush of abortions following Valentine's Day. Suzy will still be able to do her therapy in the evenings at the Bernard Evans Youth Centre and will do phone counselling while she is on the campaign trail.

Grandpa Clegg called to mourn the loss of an 'ancient tradition'. I pointed out that he had bought pants instead of marching in London and he said he was keeping the rural economy afloat and saving Cornwall from the evil grasp of Europe. I said that £3.99 was not going to turn around the Cornish economy and anyway, the pants probably came from China. He said would I rather he spent £10 in Marks & Spencer in Truro, and what did it matter if the pants gave good support and aeration? At which point I had to call for Mum as the thought of Grandpa Clegg's aerating pants was too much.

Saturday 19
Took James into town on pretext of mind-expanding trip to library but in reality to lurk outside Goddard's again. Justin was elbow deep in mince. I think I love him. I will wait for ever if that is what it takes to have his muscular, mince-stained arms around me.

Sunday 20
Grandpa came for his home visit with Treena. Why does she need to accompany him? It's not like he needs any extra caring for at our house. He only eats and watches telly. Mum was visibly put out. Especially when Treena said her peas were all vinegary and had Mum checked the sell-by. Mum smiled as if talking to a three year old or someone in Criminals and Retards and said they were capers.

Monday 21

There is a sex scandal in 9 Hopwood-White. Thin Kylie came back from Formentera with a badge of unknown provenance. (How can they afford to go on so many holidays? Her stepdad is a plasterer and her mum does Ann Summers parties. We have been abroad once—to Normandy, and we had to drive there and James was travel sick eleven times on the ferry.) The badge is of Kenzie. Mark Lambert has chucked her. He says she is a badge slut.

Tuesday 22

It was a false alarm. Apparently the badge came free with four Hooch bottle tops. Kylie brought in the CD that came with it as evidence. She and Mark were reunited (quite revoltingly) behind the mobile science lab at first break.

Wednesday 23

Watched *Jamie's School Dinners*. He is a legend in Saffron Walden as he used to live near here. The only other famous people are Marlon off *Emmerdale* and a McGann brother. Jamie Oliver should visit John Major High School. Mrs Brain's idea of nutrition is apple doughnuts. Thank God Mum was busy at her evening class (conversational French for the over-forties). She would be writing to the Prime Minister by now.

Thursday 24

Scarlet and Sad Ed saw *Jamie's School Dinners* as well. At
lunch Scarlet asked Mrs Brain how much she spent on
ingredients. She said she didn't use ingredients, it all got
sent in giant trays from Chelmsford. Then Scarlet wanted
to see the packaging for the veggie nuggets (the Stones
are strict vegetarians) to check for transfats and
monosodium glutamate but Mrs Brain said it had been
put in the giant bins next to the lower school playground
(aka Rat Corner). So Scarlet demanded statutory fresh
vegetables. Mrs Brain said she could have chips, baked
beans, or spaghetti hoops. Scarlet was about to point out
that spaghetti hoops did not, in fact, contribute to the
recommended five-a-day but Mrs Brain pointed her
bean-encrusted spoon menacingly at us so we got pizza
and Alphabites before they sold out.

When I got home, Jamie Oliver was all over the
Walden Chronicle under the headline 'Local Hero Gets
Turkey Twizzlers in a Twist'. Mum is bound to get
interested.

Friday 25

Scarlet is boycotting school meals. She has brought in
hummus sandwiches and is trying to rally support for
change. She will not have much success. There was
resistance when Fruesli bars turned up in the Coke and
crisp machine. Mr Wilmott had to get the vending

company to put back King Size Mars bars after Stacey O'Grady threatened to riot.

. . . .

Saturday 26

Went to WHSmith and bought Dad a DVD of Great Golfing Moments (his birthday is on Monday). I do not understand golf. Scarlet says it is an evil misogynistic sport perpetuated by Pringle-clad clones in Audis. She is probably right. Mum is only allowed in the clubhouse after three on a Saturday and then only if she is wearing a knee-length skirt or culottes.

. . . .

Sunday 27

Grandpa is in trouble with Mrs Peason for persistent abuse of the emergency buzzer system. He has used it to complain about loss of reception during *Neighbours*, to demand a bottle of stout, and to ask who played Bergerac in the eponymously titled TV series (during *Who Wants to be a Millionaire*). He insists they were all emergencies but Mrs Peason has put him on a written warning. Mum has told Dad to talk to him about his rebellious behaviour. She is worried he will be sent the same way as the dog.

. . . .

Monday 28

Dad's birthday. He got Great Golfing Moments (me), a golf club (Mum), a packet of three novelty golf balls

(James), and a tee holder (the dog). Officially he is forty-one. But James pointed out that really he is only ten because his birthday is actually on February 29th and so, by rights, he should only have a birthday every four years. He is a stickler for rules. He gets it from Mum. I think Dad was glad he was going to work.

Tuesday 1

St David's Day

Mum has cancelled her French conversation evening class so she can watch Jamie Oliver tomorrow. I fear the worst.

Wednesday 2

The predictable has happened. Mum, along with half the country, has gone Jamie mad. I watched her face throughout. It was all contorted like a Scream mask. She asked me if we had Turkey Twizzlers on the menu at school. I said yes, but that I didn't eat them (they are sold out by the time we get to the front of the queue). She said that is not the point and has written to Mr Wilmott demanding their immediate removal from the school premises, along with a rethink of the school catering contract. She has drawn up a suggested menu. It includes pasta, fresh fish, and risotto. Mrs Brain struggles with Bachelor's Savoury Rice.

I offered to hand deliver the letter for her tomorrow (i.e. put it in bin) but she says she will do it herself. She is not bothering with St Regina's primary. James takes sandwiches after a stand-off over some roast pork and apple sauce.

Thursday 3

Left the house early before Mum could try to walk me to school. She wears a cagoule, which is a criminal offence at John Major High.

With any luck the letter will be lost in the school office for years. Mrs Leech, the school secretary (bad hair; too much face powder; biscuit habit) is notoriously bad at filing. She once lost all Year Eleven's GCSE results under a tin of assorted shortbread.

Friday 4

Watched *Bring It On* on DVD tonight while Mum and Dad played gin rummy at Clive and Marjory's. Scarlet had to smuggle it in inside the case for *Harry Potter*—Mum would never have let it in the house.

Why can't we do cheerleading in PE instead of hockey? Since the school sold off the playing fields to be turned into executive housing we have to do games on the sheep field, which is fraught with dangers like the electric fence and sheep poo.

Saturday 5

Got Mum a Mother's Day card in WHSmith. It has a picture of a single daffodil on the front. It took a long time to choose it. Mum does not like cards involving whimsical kittens, puppies, overambitious floral arrangements, rude jokes, or nudity in any form. Also got her a box of Black Magic. Scarlet did not get anything for Suzy, as Suzy says every day should be a celebration of motherhood, it should not be reduced to a single Sunday, a mass-produced card, and a box of cheap chocolates. Felt guilty about the Black Magic, but Mum doesn't like Thornton's Continental since they changed the packaging.

Sunday 6
Mothering Sunday

Gave Mum her WHSmith card and Black Magic. James gave her a painted pottery ashtray he made at school. Mum had to pretend to be pleased and said she would use it as an olive dish, but I could sense she was planning a letter to St Regina's to complain about them encouraging smoking.

Scarlet came over to escape her house. Neither she nor Jack had got Suzy anything and Suzy had locked herself in the home office and was playing Suzanne Vega albums at full volume. Mum let us eat a layer of Black Magic. I hope she wasn't feigning delight at my present as well.

Monday 7

Mrs Leech has clearly tidied up her act. I fear Mum's Jamie Oliver frenzy letter has reached Mr Wilmott after all and that he is putting pressure on Mrs Brain to amend her saturated-fat-focused menu. There were bananas (brown) on offer for pudding next to the chocolate sponge and pink custard.

Tuesday 8

Mr Wilmott has definitely shopped me to Mrs Brain. She gave me a very shrivelled sausage and only five chips for lunch. I am going to have to join Scarlet and her hummus sandwich rally if this goes on.

Wednesday 9

Today is the anniversary of Fat Kylie's dad's fatal encounter with a Findus Crispy Pancake. She had a letter to get off games. Considering the way in which he died and Kylie's veering towards childhood obesity this seems highly inappropriate.

I asked Miss Vicar (stick-thin; no breasts; facial hair) and Miss Beadle (overweight; bulgy eyes like Joey in *Friends* or rabbits with myxomatosis) if we could do cheerleading like in *Bring It On*. They have clearly seen the film, possibly several times, as Miss Beadle said: 'This is not California and you are not Kirsten Dunst. Now stop shivering and partner up with a netball.'

Got burnt nuggets (possibly chicken, but with the flavour of pork) and an odd-tasting yoghurt for lunch. Am definitely bringing sandwiches tomorrow.

Thursday 10

Was sick four times in the night. It was the yoghurt. Mrs Brain is poisoning me to make me pay for Mum's letter. Mum demanded a vomit sample for laboratory inspection but I flushed it away and got out the Cillit Bang before she could take a swab. I do not want to aggravate Mrs Brain further.

Lay on the sofa sipping Evian and watching daytime telly. Why, oh why, do we not have satellite? Actually, I know the answer to that and it is because it is on Mum's proscribed list due to *a*) cost and *b*) shopping and porn channels and *c*) excessive sport. *This Morning* has definitely gone downhill. It is all about sex and angels. Even the dog got up and left.

Friday 11

My so-called life, as I know it, is over! We are moving to London! Dad has been offered a new job but he has to start in a month. He and Mum are going house and school hunting on Monday in a place called Dulwich. It is bound to be full of gangsters and ASBOs. I cannot wait to tell Scarlet. I will be devastated to leave her and Sad Ed behind, but they can come and see me in the holidays and meet all my black friends and we can hang out on the King's Road or the giant Topshop. Maybe I will have a leaving party and Justin will confess his true feelings for me.

Granny and Grandpa Clegg are coming to look after us while Mum and Dad house hunt. Last time they came Granny Clegg let James ride round into town in her wicker shopping trolley. I hope she does not bring it this time.

Had cheese and tomato sandwich at lunch. Am not risking the wrath of Mrs Brain again. I expect my school in London will have a multicultural menu like rice and peas and healthy lentil daal. I will not have to eat shrivelled sausage and life-threatening yoghurt again.

. . . .

Saturday 12
Dulwich is not a ghetto. It is an upper-middle-class suburb and is where Margaret Thatcher and Tom Cruise have houses. James googled it. But on the plus side it is very close to Peckham and has an above-average car-crime and burglary problem.

. . . .

Sunday 13
Granny and Grandpa Clegg have arrived. They got a bus all the way from Newquay to Stansted Airport where Dad picked them up. The shopping trolley was thankfully too big for the luggage compartment on the coach. They have just brought Spar bags instead.

Grandpa Clegg says he does not understand why we want to go and live in a city that is being overrun by 'gyppos and darkies' (he means asylum seekers and Muslims) thanks to Tony Blair. James told him he was being racist but Grandpa Clegg said he couldn't be racist

64

because his grandfather was a midget. He is a racist. He thinks Saffron Walden is dangerously exotic. But compared to St Slaughter it is. We have the Hassans; the Hangs, who run the Mandarin Palace; Ying from the Siam Smile; Mrs Wong the sadistic dentist; plus some Asian families on the Whiteshot estate. The closest Grandpa gets to a foreigner is the Australian barmaid in Truro, and he thinks she should be deported.

Was not allowed to go to Scarlet's due to presence of Cleggs so that is another episode of *The O.C.* that I will never get to enjoy.

Monday 14

Commonwealth Day

Mum and Dad left after breakfast. Granny Clegg insisted on walking me to school. I told her this was not necessary but she said I could get mugged or raped or run over and she didn't want to have to explain that to my mother. She seemed alarmed to see Ali Hassan and the Wongs walking in the gates and clutched her Spar bag tightly to her chest. God knows what she thinks they are going to do. Grandpa Clegg took James so it could have been worse. He has been known to feign a Chinese accent at inappropriate moments.

Told Scarlet about London. She is devastated and is going to organize a leaving party at her house. Then I told Ms Hopwood-White who announced it to the class. Fat

Kylie cheered but Ms Hopwood-White gave her an immediate detention. Mark Lambert said he was a cockney. Then he tried to prove it by stabbing himself with his compasses and yelling that there was 'claret all over the gaff'. He is not a cockney. He is from Braintree.

When I got home Granny Clegg had fed all the Waitrose pasta sauce, asparagus, and half-fat fromage frais to the dog and replaced it with Fray Bentos pies and Viennetta. Granny Clegg only serves sandwiches, cold meats, and ready-meals. This is since the mythical occasion on which she Tried to Make Rice Pudding and forgot the rice, so we had to eat boiled milk skin. (She won't throw anything away—it is her working-class upbringing. Mum is the same, she will store half a leftover boiled potato in Tupperware for a week rather than waste it. The dog always gets it in the end, though.)

My room smells of Fray Bentos and liniment. I have lit one of the incense sticks that Scarlet got at the Cambridge Folk Festival last year to get rid of it.

Tuesday 15

Mum rang before school. Granny Clegg has reported me for smoking drugs. I told her it was incense to banish the smell of Fray Bentos and old person. She told me not to do anything new-fangled with Granny Clegg in the house. That includes using the internet and microwave or talking about iPods.

Nine Hopwood-White has gone London-mad. Mark Lambert is now talking in rhyming slang and the Kylies think they are black. They are calling each other 'nigger' and 'girlfriend'. It is pathetic.

Wednesday 16
There has been a terrible accident. Granny Clegg let James put food colouring in his bath. I pointed out the dangers of E-numbers but she said she had drunk blue milk for fun when she was little and it hadn't done her any harm (this is the limit of things to do for amusement in Cornwall). But then she left James unsupervised while she went to check the Fray Bentos and he added the entire bottle and now he is tinged yellow. Granny has showered him three times but it will not come off. He will have to go to school like it. I hope for Granny Clegg's sake that it has worn off by Friday when Mum and Dad get home.

Thursday 17
St Patrick's Day. Holiday (N. Ire.)
James got sent home from school with suspected jaundice. Granny Clegg explained the food colouring thing but Reverend Begley, the head teacher, said it would cause a panic among the other parents and he didn't want a health scare on his hands.

I suggested Granny Clegg should try to dull it down a bit by giving him a bath in another colour. But the Co-op only had blue (Granny Clegg will not shop at Waitrose) so now James is green. Mum is going to go mad. They are back tomorrow. I cannot wait to find out what my new school is like. I wonder if they scan you for guns and knives when you go through the gates.

Friday 18

Change of plan. We are not moving to London. Mum and Dad got back looking very angry and weary. The only houses they could afford were in a place called Tulse Hill, which Mum said she recognized from several reports on *News at Ten*. There were no places at the girls' grammar either. The only school she could get me into was Peckham Academy and that only had a place because one of their Year Nines was pregnant *again* and the pupil crèche wasn't opening for three years and Dad refused to pay for me to go private on principle when there was a perfectly good school place for me in Saffron Walden (he does not come to parents' evenings). Dad is going to stay at his old job. So my life is once more one of middle-class market-town misery. Grandpa Clegg is overjoyed. He sees it as a victory against Tony Blair.

Rang Scarlet to tell her. I thought she would be happy I was staying but she is annoyed at having to cancel the leaving party. I asked her to come over but she said she would be too busy apologizing to the caterers (Suzy).

Mum is so pleased at not having to move to London she did not even tell Granny Clegg off for James looking like an alien. But then she asked where her manuka honey had gone and Granny Clegg said she had thought it was off and had given it to the dog. Mum said it cost her £7 a pot and Granny Clegg said the dog was clearly undernourished and that if Mum couldn't look after it then she would be happy to rehome it at Bellevue. James started crying but Mum said he was in no position to complain because he was green. So that is it. The dog is moving to Cornwall. I hope it knows what it is letting itself in for.

. . . .

Saturday 19

The dog has gone. Mum is visibly relieved. I think it was costing her a fortune in cleaning products. She won't be so calm when Grandpa Riley finds out. He hasn't spoken to Granny and Grandpa Clegg since an argument about Terry Wogan in 1985. James has shut himself in his room and is talking Elvish, presumably to his Elijah Wood poster—I don't think Des Lynam or Will Young look like hobbit fans.

I don't understand all this worry over the dog, when we should all be mourning the fact that we are stuck in Saffron Walden instead of trudging the mean streets of

London. Scarlet said we should try to make Saffron Walden more urban and edgy. So we tried hanging around the bus shelter like disenfranchised youths. But we got bored after an hour and went to Eaden Lilley's for smoothies.

Sunday 20

Palm Sunday
First day of spring

James has an imaginary friend called Mumtaz. At breakfast Mum asked him if he was feeling better and he said, 'Only Mumtaz understands me.' Mum (who has been glued to *Supernanny*) said we should humour him and treat Mumtaz as if she were real until he has got over the trauma of the dog moving.

Monday 21

James is back at school. The green has finally worn off his face so, unless he has PE, he will pass Reverend Begley's colour test. He asked if Mumtaz could come for tea on his birthday on Thursday. Mum smiled through gritted teeth and said she could and asked what she liked to eat. He said Shreddies and Marmite soldiers. These are James's favourite foods. I have never had an imaginary friend. Sad Ed says he had one called Geoffrey who wore a suit and read Enid Blyton books. I asked him when Geoffrey had gone and he said two years ago, when he briefly got into death metal. Apparently the noise was too much. At this rate we will have Mumtaz for years.

Told Ms Hopwood-White I was not moving to London. Thin Kylie booed so Ms Hopwood-White sent her to see Mr Wilmott. Mark Lambert said it was because I didn't have cockney blood like him and anyway my Bristols were too small. So Ms Hopwood-White sent him to see Mr Wilmott as well. They have been given detention for a week because Mrs Leech caught them groping on C corridor while they waited for punishment.

Tuesday 22
James has ordered Mum to purchase a present for Mumtaz as it is her birthday on Friday. He says they can have a joint party so they will need two cakes as well, and two kinds of jelly. Mum is beginning to regret her decision to humour him. I predict Mumtaz will be sent packing by Thursday night.

Wednesday 23
Went into town to get James a present. Mum wearily told me to get something for Mumtaz so I got her a Beach Babe Barbie for £12.99. Mum said it was a bit much to spend on a figment of James's imagination but Dad said, 'What price sanity?' and I pointed out she could take it

back next week once James had got over her. Got James a laminator. He has wanted one for ages. God knows what he will do with it.

* * *

Thursday 24
Maundy Thursday
James's birthday

Mumtaz is real! It is Mr Patel's niece who arrived from Birmingham three months ago. This is typical. Why does James get to have a best friend of colour? I tried to befriend Ali Hassan once but he said he would rather I didn't talk to him about *The O.C.* as it was meaningless American propaganda. Also, he is in the maths club, which is sad.

James got the laminator, a cereal selection pack containing forbidden Frosties (Grandpa Riley), a *Lord of the Rings* calendar (last year's) (Granny and Grandpa Clegg), a Jesus Loves Me car sticker (Auntie Joyless), and a season ticket to Mole Hall wildlife park (sum total of wildlife: ten marmosets and an otter) (Mum and Dad). He has laminated all his pictures of Elijah Wood. Mumtaz was delighted with her Barbie. Mum glared at Dad. He hid behind the *Walden Chronicle*, which was leading on the under-fives Easter bonnet competition. It is so unfair. If we were in London our local paper would be full of shoot-outs and gang wars.

* * *

Friday 25

Good Friday

No school.

The Barbie is back. Mumtaz's dad came round this morning and said he didn't want Mumtaz being corrupted by the Western lack of respect for women and money. Mum is livid. She can't take it back now as there is jelly on Barbie's bikini. Also, James has laminated the receipt.

. . . .

Saturday 26

Dad is beside himself with delight because something called *Dr Who* starts on telly tonight. He says James and I will be scared out of our wits and will be hiding behind the sofa. Mum said if it was that traumatic the BBC wouldn't put it on at 6.35. I don't know what the fuss is about. If it is anything like *Dr Quinn, Medicine Woman* it will be so rubbish that no one will watch it anyway.

8 p.m.

Mum is writing to the BBC to complain about screening *Dr Who* before the 9 p.m. watershed. It was not like *Dr Quinn, Medicine Woman*. James was so shocked that he dropped his milk all over the sofa. Dad's viewing was suspended while Mum washed it off before it went sour.

I may well write to the BBC as well, as there were some serious flaws in their plot, like how will Billie Piper wash her clothes on the Tardis? By the end of the series she will be like Mrs Simpson. No one in telly thinks of these things. Like in *24* (which I watched illegally at Scarlet's)—no one went to the loo for a whole day, when, in reality, with all that excitement, they would be queueing up for a wee.

Sunday 27
Easter Day
British Summer Time begins
10 a.m.
Got five Easter eggs: one Green and Black's Organic (Mum and Dad); one wooden with a picture of Jesus on the cross (Auntie Joyless); one Creme Egg (James); one KitKat (Grandpa and Treena—what is she doing giving me eggs?); and one Smarties, sell-by date last April (Granny Clegg). Am going to ration them. Only small children and Fat Kylie eat all their Easter eggs on Easter Sunday.

4 p.m.
Have eaten all eggs. Sad Ed came over and said it was better to do things by extreme in this life and to eat it all in one go. He had already eaten a giant Dairy Milk and two Lindt rabbits. Felt so sick that we could not even make it to Scarlet's. Had to lie on the bed groaning instead. Also, Ed has chipped a tooth trying to eat Auntie

Joyless's wooden biblical egg. Next year I will nibble only 70 per cent cocoa solids dark chocolate a square a day, no matter what Ed says.

. . . .

Monday 28
Easter Monday

There is nothing to do in Saffron Walden on a bank holiday. If we had moved to London I could have gone to Harrods or Topshop. Here only Mr Patel's and the DFS on the Bishop's Stortford ring road are open. So I am OK if I want a sherbet dib-dab, a pornographic magazine, or a leather sofa.

Went round Scarlet's. Suzy was busy plotting her election campaign. She is sure Tony Blair is going to announce it next week. The kitchen was full of Labour Party members drinking lattes and phoning people up on their BlackBerries. Bob had been called into work for a complicated breech birth. Suzy said that the baby's bottom was lodged in the vaginal canal. So me and Scarlet left before she got more graphic. What is a vaginal canal? It sounds horrible. We went for a boat trip down the canal in Northampton once and we saw a shopping trolley and two dead pigeons in the water.

Scarlet had also eaten all her Easter eggs. She says she is full of self-loathing. She thinks we should become anorexic for a bit because it is a rite of passage for any prospective goth or tragic literary person. She is right.

75

Lots of famous and brilliant people are anorexic. Suzy had made Nigella's melting chocolate puddings for tea so we are going to wait until next week to try it.

- -

Tuesday 29

Grandpa has been ordered to leave the Pink Geranium sheltered housing unit. He has been given until Saturday to pack his things. Mum says he is not coming to live here, not over her dead body. Dad is going to see Mrs Peason after work to reconcile their differences.

8 p.m.

Grandpa is moving in with us, temporarily, until Mum can find him suitable accommodation. He has caused a scandal amongst the elderly citizens of the Pink Geranium by having an affair with his care worker, Treena. Apparently they have been doing it since February. Grandpa insists he is the victim of an ageist hate campaign but Mrs Peason said he had been caught with his trousers down, literally, and that it was not a pretty sight. Mum is in shock. Not only is there a forty-five-year age gap but Treena is from Bolton. I think Dad is secretly jealous. Treena is younger than Mum and she wears a Wonderbra. Personally, I am on Mum's side. At least her nails are real.

- -

Wednesday 30

Told Scarlet about Grandpa Riley. She says it is a classic Lolita complex. Suzy said Grandpa should be careful in case he has a heart attack in the middle of relations. She said ambulance men had to rescue one of her patients last year when her eighty-two-year-old husband died mid-session. He was wearing handcuffs at the time and had to be sawn loose.

Thursday 31

James has laminated the contents of Mum's purse. Mum went to use a £20 note in Waitrose but the cashier said she couldn't accept it as it might be a clever ploy to disguise fake currency. Mum demanded to see the manager. He agreed with the cashier and confiscated the plastic £20 note pending police investigation. Mum says she will be glad when the school holidays are over.

april

Friday 1

April Fool's Day

9 a.m.

It is Anorexia Day. Scarlet and I are going to start starvation this morning. I ate two bowls of Shreddies to prepare. Sad Ed is going to invigilate in case we get hypoglycaemic and try to binge on bourbons.

12 p.m.

This is easy. We have drunk three cans of Diet Coke each and eaten some toothpaste. Scarlet says your breath smells when you are anorexic. I am not hungry at all.

2 p.m.

Sad Ed has eaten three portions of Suzy's lentil moussaka and a bag of Cheetos he had brought for an emergency. My stomach is rumbling. But I will not give in. The Olsen twins did not get where they are by eating Cheetos.

4 p.m.

We have finished the toothpaste.

5 p.m.

I feel faint. Scarlet is very quiet.

7 p.m.

It is all over. Suzy came in with a Waitrose pizza. We are

81

not cut out to be anorexics. Sad Ed says we can try out alcoholism in a few years instead.

Saturday 2

Went to pick Grandpa up from the Pink Geranium sheltered housing complex. He was standing outside with his suitcases and Mrs Peason, looking sorrowful (Grandpa, not Mrs Peason—she looked triumphant). There was no sign of Treena. Mrs Peason said, 'Never in all my years have I come across such a poorly behaved pensioner. He is more of a menace than that dog.'

When we got back, Grandpa asked where the dog was so he could be reunited with the only living thing that cared about him. Mum said it had broken all its house rules and had been sent to Cornwall to live with her mother. Grandpa said the dog would pine itself to death living with those two inbreds (Granny and Grandpa Clegg) and demanded its safe return forthwith. Mum said he was in no position to make demands (I notice she did not correct him calling Granny and Grandpa Clegg inbreds). So Grandpa has shut himself in the spare room and is smoking Benson and Hedges. Mum has festooned the landing with Glade plug-ins but I guarantee she will cave in before Grandpa does.

3 p.m.

Grandpa is victorious. He got all teary and said that both

he and the dog were on their last legs and one of them would probably die in the next few months. I don't think this is true but Mum felt guilty and has agreed to let it return, provided that Grandpa keeps it under strict control and that smoking is confined to the back garden in the dark so that the neighbours can't see. Dad is going to drive to Cornwall tomorrow to fetch it. He is not happy, it is a twelve hour round trip. James is going with him. He is taking his Elvish book and a packet of digestives as a welcome home present.

Sunday 3

The dog is home. It is sitting on the sofa next to Grandpa eating Werther's Originals. Dad is in bed. James made him listen to *Lord of the Rings*, as read by Stephen Fry, for twelve hours and the dog was sick on the M25. Also Granny and Grandpa Clegg did not give the dog up without a fight. They want visiting rights.

The Pope is dead. I do not see what all the fuss is about. He was very old and they can pick another one.

Monday 4

The Pope's death was more significant than I thought. Fat Kylie and her many brothers and sisters are off school. Maybe I should become religious. You get loads of concessions.

Tuesday 5

The election has been declared. It is on May 5th. Ms Hopwood-White let us watch the news at lunchtime. She is running mock elections at school. Mark Lambert said he was going to organize an Anarchist Party. Sad Ed said 'How anachronistic.' And Mark Lambert said, 'No, anarchist, you deaf retard.' So Ms Hopwood-White sent him to Mr Wilmott.

Fat Kylie was back in school. She had a note for Mr Wilmott saying that she needed to be able to sip Coca-Cola throughout the day to keep her strength up at this traumatic time. Even Mr Wilmott is too scared of Fat Kylie to say no.

There was an anti-Hugo Thorndyke leaflet on the doormat when I got home. Scarlet says Suzy says 'going negative' is the only way she will win in this town. She is hoping a sex scandal will rear its ugly head. Scarlet is worried it could all backfire. If Hugo Thorndyke goes negative on Suzy the results could be disastrous. She has heaps of skeletons in her closet including a lesbian experience and hallucinogenic drugs.

Wednesday 6

Fat Kylie could not do PE because of the Pope. Miss Beadle said that she had better be over it by next Wednesday or she would put her on the school hockey team. They are crap and always lose and it means you have to go to school on Saturday.

Mum has banned Grandpa and the dog from excessive daytime telly and biscuits. They were getting through four packets of Gypsy Creams during *LK Today*, *The Jeremy Kyle Show*, *This Morning*, *Neighbours*, *Doctors*, and *Murder She Wrote*. She is enrolling him at the Twilight Years Day Centre, starting on Monday. Grandpa says he will be forced to make raffia owls by over-jolly do-gooders and that the tedium could kill him. I think Mum is hoping this is the case.

Thursday 7

Suzy is in trouble with Labour Party headquarters for her anti-Hugo leaflet. They have written her another one all about extra nurses and tax credits for poor people. It has a picture of the whole family on it, but it has been doctored to make Jack's hair shorter and get rid of Scarlet's goth make-up.

Friday 8

Election fever is sweeping school. Jack is going to be the mock Labour candidate. He is standing against Ali Hassan (Conservative), Pippa Newbold (Lib Dem) and Oona Rickets (Green Party/Lesbian and Gay Alliance/Stop the War). Ms Hopwood-White has banned the BNP from fielding a candidate.

Sad Ed says he is not voting because tragic geniuses are above such a cheap media circus. He is right. I will abstain.

I bet Julie Burchill doesn't vote. She will be too busy enjoying lesbian sex on Brighton beach.

8 p.m.
Scarlet rang to say that Justin is going to be Jack's campaign manager. I have volunteered to help with leaflets.

Saturday 9
Charles and Camilla got married today. Grandpa is outraged. He is still mourning Princess Diana. He says he doesn't blame the Queen staying away from the service. Dad said that, no matter what the Queen thought, she should still have turned up. But Grandpa pointed out that he had a hard job persuading Grandma Riley to turn up at the church when Dad married a Clegg. Luckily Mum was busy descaling the kettle and didn't hear him.

Sunday 10
The dog has done a poo in Clive and Marjory's tulips. It was poking out of one of the flowers. Grandpa said it was an artistic triumph and James took a photo to send to the local paper's 'Fancy That' competition page but Mum says it could jeopardize her dog-poo campaign and deleted the picture and cleared the poo up before Marjory noticed. It has left a smear on the petals. I

hope Marjory does not cut the flowers for the dining table.

Monday 11

Mum's Day Centre plan has backfired. It turns out that Treena has got a job there after being sacked by Mrs Peason for sexual misdemeanours. Grandpa is jubilant. He says his flames of passion are rekindled. So Mum and I left the room before he got any more graphic.

Tuesday 12

Went round to Scarlet's after school to help plan Jack's campaign. He is having to use his bedroom as Suzy has taken over the kitchen, cellar, and second bathroom for her campaign. It is painted black. I am going to ask Mum if I can paint my room black. I am too old for stencils of ladybirds.

Justin and Sophie were both there as well. She laughed and said, 'Oh God, the peanut girl,' and tossed her Barbie-blonde hair so that it swished in Justin's face. Jack told her to shut up and that he needed all the help he could get in the fight against fascism (Ali Hassan and the maths club geeks). Ha. She won't be laughing when I am snogging Justin at the victory party in the lower school canteen.

Jack said he is veering towards a Marxist campaign. Justin agreed and said that Karl Marx could well be the key to cracking the impressionable lower school as well as the über-left anti-Blairite upper sixth. Who is Marx? I am going to have to politicize myself fast.

Asked Mum if I could paint my room black. She said she would compromise on magnolia, apple white, or butterscotch. I do not think they are much of a compromise.

Wednesday 13

Went to the library at lunchtime. The hairy librarian Mr Knox said the only Marx they had was in the video section. It is a film called *Duck Soup*. I said that would do.

Watched the film with Grandpa after school. He said it is a cinematic classic. He laughed so hard he said he had nearly wet himself. I don't know which one is Karl. Probably the one that looks like Robert Winston. He seemed to be in charge. I do not see the political relevance. It must be subliminal, like in Pringles adverts, which make you eat the whole tube. But Justin is right, the madcap humour could win over Year Seven and some of the more idiotic sixth formers. I will take the video to tomorrow's campaign strategy meeting. I bet Sophie hasn't done any research.

Thursday 14

Karl Marx is not one of the Marx brothers, as Justin pointed out after he, Jack, and Sophie had finished rolling round the floor in hysterics. That is the last time I use Mr Knox as a reference tool. I shall only use Google from now on. It is infallible. Except that time me and Sad Ed tried to find the Waterboys' official fanpage and got a disturbing website about men weeing on each other. Jack said that I was a perfect example of the depoliticization of today's youth and that I was exactly why this election was so necessary, to get people to stop worrying about *I'm A Celebrity* and start worrying about big brother (they are doing *Nineteen Eighty-Four* for GCSE and all think they are living in a fascist police state). Sophie said that should be their slogan and Justin agreed. Sophie is a hypocrite. I know for a fact that she voted seventeen times for Jordan last year. Then Justin started to do a Groucho Marx/ Robert Winston impression and they all got hysterics again so me and Scarlet went down to the cellar to help Suzy telephone-canvass disillusioned former Labour voters (all forty-five of them) instead.

Jack came down later and said, 'Sorry, Riley.' But Scarlet told him we are going to work for a real politician (i.e. Suzy) from now on, unless he disbars Sophie from the campaign. Jack asked on what grounds and Scarlet said on blondeness and idiocy. Jack said you can't get rid of someone on the grounds of them being blonde and idiotic and Scarlet said what about Anthea Turner and Jack had to agree. But he is still not going to sack her because Microwave Muffins are sponsoring their posters.

Friday 15

Treena is in Grandpa's bedroom. James says he brought her back from the Day Centre along with a raffia owl (now hanging on the downstairs toilet wall). He says he has not been able to ascertain what is going on in the room due to Neil Diamond being played at high volume but there is possibly sex happening because at one point the dog got shooed out and Grandpa was only wearing a string vest, pants, and socks. I said Treena might be giving him a therapeutic massage for his arthritis. But James said Treena was in her bra and that no one got arthritis 'down there'. (How does James know about things like this? I blame the internet. Mum should put stricter parental controls on it. It still allows access to medical sites.) I asked James where Mum was and why she was allowing this activity to go on, and he said she had called Dad back from work as a matter of emergency and was now Cillit Banging the downstairs loo to block out the horror.

4.30 p.m.

Dad has cautioned Mum over the use of term 'emergency'. Mum says it is an emergency when there are impressionable children in the house. (I hope she is not talking about me. I am not likely to want to go out and snog old men or northern care workers after witnessing Grandpa and Treena's sexploits. And James is only interested in male celebrities and fictitious midgets.) Grandpa said he can't go to Treena's house in case Kelly next door sees him and tells her husband who is in prison with Treena's husband Des for the same attempted burglary. Mum has compromised. Grandpa is only allowed conjugal visits at pre-arranged times when all under-fourteens can be supervised in a distracting activity. Grandpa says Mum is worse than Mrs Peason. He is right. At least Mrs Peason did not ban Ribena.

Saturday 16

Granny and Grandpa Clegg rang to check up on 'Valerie'. I assume they mean the dog. It must be named after Valerie Singleton, their all-time favourite TV presenter (now a lesbian, but this news does not seem to have reached Cornwall yet). I told them 'he' was fine. I asked how Granny Clegg was and she said she was sick of all the canvassers. Apparently the Lib Dem candidate for Redruth had asked for her vote earlier. He won't get it. She does not approve of Charles Kennedy. Her motto in life is 'Never trust anyone ginger or with a beard. Or, worse, with a ginger beard.' I asked her if she had considered voting Labour but she said, 'Not likely. That Gordon Brown has no neck and greasy hair. You'd think that Sarah would buy him some Vosene.' I pointed out that Gordon Brown was not the leader of the Labour Party and she said, 'That's what you think.' (What does she know, I wonder?) She and Grandpa Clegg are voting UKIP.

Told Grandpa Riley about Valerie. He said no dog of his was going round with a name like that and what was wrong with 'dog'? Dad said we should have a vote on it and that we could all put a name in a hat (actually a large Tupperware container). I put in 'Byron' after the romantic poet.

The dog is called Frodo. It got off lightly. Mum had put in 'Jeremy', as in Paxman.

Sunday 17

Went round Scarlet's. Jack was there with Sophie and Justin. Sophie's dad has printed a hundred 'Turn off *I'm A Celebrity* and tune in to big brother' posters. They have the Microwave Muffins logo at the bottom. Scarlet pointed out that they didn't actually say 'Vote Labour' anywhere on them but Sophie tutted and said the message was implicit. I think she may have overestimated the electorate at John Major High.

Monday 18

Jack's election campaign has been derailed. The 'Turn off *I'm A Celebrity* and tune in to big brother' posters have caused confusion. Most people seem to think it is an anti-ITV campaign by Sean Cummings in Year Twelve, whose mum is an accountant at Channel 4. Mr Wilmott has made Lou the caretaker (formerly of Mrs Duddy's Criminals and Retards) take the posters down, as commercial advertising is banned from school premises.

This debacle has cost Jack dearly. The maths club, who are doing daily polls, are putting Pippa Newbold in the lead, down to her free Chomp bars at first break.

Scarlet says Jack has considered sacking Sophie, but that her dad has promised to sponsor T-shirts and free jolly bugs. Sad Ed said he should have more principles but Scarlet said electioneering isn't about principles it is about rich donors and celebrity endorsements.

That is it. I am going to get a celebrity to endorse Jack. Then Justin will be thanking me not Sophie Microwave Muffins Jacobs.

. . . .

Tuesday 19

Grandpa got a letter today from the hospital informing him that his grommet operation has been cancelled. He says the NHS is going down the pan and that no one cares about pensioners any more and that people like him fought in two wars to put people like Tony Blair in Downing Street instead of Helmut Kohl. Mum pointed out that Grandpa was only seven when the Second World War started. Grandpa was about to reply but Mum's lips went super thin and she did that glary thing with her eyes so he went to take the dog for a walk instead. When he got back he was happy again though. He said he had met a very nice man on the street who had listened to all his problems and agreed with him about the NHS. Mum asked him his name. It is Hugo

Thorndyke, evil Conservative MP for Saffron Walden and environs.

. . . .

Wednesday 20

The election is inescapable. James has joined the Conservative Party, the Liberal Democrats, the Green Party, and Veritas. He says he is keeping his options open. The only party that has not accepted him into its ranks is Labour. You'd think they would want all the support they could get, even from an eight-year-old hobbit obsessive. I said I didn't think he was allowed to sign up until he was of voting age. He said he had used a false name and age, i.e. Grandpa's. I said that was identity theft but he said it was in a good cause because he is going to campaign to get the voting age lowered. I don't think that primary school children should be allowed to vote. Mum doesn't think anyone should be allowed to vote unless they have passed an intelligence test. That would rule out all the O'Gradys and possibly Granny and Grandpa Clegg.

The dog is not responding to its new name. I tried to get it to stop chewing Mum's *Woman and Home* magazine by saying, 'Down, Frodo,' in a commanding but loving voice as recommended by my dog training book. But it totally ignored me and swallowed a picture of Gloria Hunniford and then Mum came in and shrieked, 'Get out of here, you hairy halfwit,' and it stopped what it was doing immediately.

. . . .

Thursday 21
Queen Elizabeth II born (1926)

Grandpa is on the front page of the local paper under the headline 'Ernest's Ear'! There is a photo of him and the dog in our living room. They are looking sadly at the camera. Grandpa is clutching his ear like it is in agony. The article says:

Ernest Riley (pictured left) has been hit by a cruel double whammy from local NHS and care services. Already reeling after being denied a place at the Pink Geranium sheltered housing unit, Ernest was knocked for six when he found out that a vital ear operation had been cancelled for the second time. Ernest says he is relying on the goodwill and patience of family members but that he fears it could run out at any time.

Local MP Hugo Thorndyke said that this showed just how low Britain's provision for pensioners had sunk at the hands of the Prime Minister. He is spearheading the campaign to get Ernest's Ear on the operating table before election day.

Mum is hopping mad. She said it makes it sound like she is going to throw him out on the street. I think she is thinking of throwing him out now. Grandpa said it wasn't his idea to be in the paper, that Hugo Thorndyke had suggested it. Then the doorbell went and it was Suzy and Scarlet. Mum does not like Suzy very much, she thinks she is too permissive, but she got the Duchy Originals out anyway, so she may be softening. Suzy flounced in in a cloud of Opium and said that Grandpa is being used as a pawn in Hugo Thorndyke's giant game of political chess. She says that Hugo Thorndyke doesn't care if Grandpa lives or dies (I didn't think grommets were life-threatening). Normally Grandpa doesn't like women in politics but Suzy was wearing a daringly low V-neck so he went all teary and let her hug him. He is so transparent.

Suzy has a weird effect on people. It must be her aura of sex counsellor. Or the large breasts. Because then Grandpa admitted to her that his operation hadn't been cancelled, that he had missed it, twice, because they had clashed with crucial storylines in *Neighbours*. Mum made him get the letter out and it was true. It was a stern warning about wasting NHS resources. Suzy is keeping it as evidence. She says Ernest's Ear is going to be the nail in the coffin of Thorndyke's campaign. Then she said she had to go because she had a meet and greet at the Golf Club and a group orgasm session at the Bernard Evans Youth Centre. I hope she doesn't get them muddled up.

Friday 22

Suzy was on Radio Cambridge this morning talking about the Ernest's Ear scandal. She says it was a typical Tory anti-NHS smear and that what Hugo Thorndyke really wanted to do was to shut down the NHS and make Grandpa pay £1,000 to get it done on BUPA instead. Then Hugo Thorndyke came on and said he had been misled by Grandpa. So Suzy asked him if he was accusing a vulnerable elderly man of lying. And then Hugo got all flustered and the presenter tried to cut in because it was time for listeners' recipes but Suzy got the microphone and shouted, 'Are you listening, Saffron Walden? Your MP is trying to get a confused seventy-three year old to shoulder the blame for his own deceit.' Then there was a crashing sound and Brenda from Royston started talking about cauliflower cheese.

Saw Jack on the way to school. He said, 'Nice hit on the Tories, Riley.' Then I remembered that I am supposed to be getting him a celebrity endorsement to lure Justin away from Sophie Jacobs so me, Scarlet, and Sad Ed decided to track one down this weekend. The choices are Marlon out of *Emmerdale* or the McGann brother. We are going to go for Marlon as none of us can remember what the McGann was in or what his name is.

Saturday 23

St George's Day

Went into town with Scarlet and Sad Ed to search for a celebrity. We have ruled out Stead and Simpson, Oxfam, New Look, the shop that has giant pants in the window, Gordon Bennett fabrics, Star Burger, Gray Palmer (no celebrities wear Aertex or tweed), and the library. The locations are: Waitrose (upmarket delicatessen shopping possibilities), Moss Bros (in case he has TV award do to go to and needs to hire a dinner suit), and Sketchleys (in case he needs to get the suit cleaned).

5 p.m.

Walked around Waitrose for two hours without seeing a single celebrity. Miss Beadle and Miss Vicar were in there buying exotic vegetables and Nutella. How can teachers afford to shop in Waitrose? I thought they were all impoverished and had to buy in bulk from Lidl or Netto. Then Sad Ed remembered that Tracey Hughes's brother, Seamus, works on the fish counter on a Saturday. He was gutting a turbot. I asked him if he had ever seen Marlon buying salmon or lobster (expensive celebrity fish) and he said that he had it on good authority (Gary Fletcher who stacks the pet food aisle) that he gets his shopping delivered. So Scarlet asked if he could get his home address but he said it was more than his job was worth. (He has an inflated sense of worth: he wears white wellies for God's sake. Anyone would think he had signed an official secrets act.) So we bought some mini Victoria sponges and came home.

Sunday 24
First Day of Passover

Grandpa is demanding to be taken to the St George's Day parade to show patriotic spirit. Mum said she had a roast to do and Dad is playing golf with Clive so I am going with James and the dog. I do not see what the fuss is about. All it involves is the Brownies and other military-style youth groups marching up the High Street to the church. It is very disappointing. One year James was in it but he has left Cubs because the religious element clashes with his Elvish tendencies.

1 p.m.
The parade was a disaster. I am too weak to relay details but to cut a long story short, Grandpa had a fight with Hugo Thorndyke and the dog savaged Marlon from *Emmerdale*. On the plus side, Hugo Thorndyke was caught on mobile phone camera by Fat Kylie who is going to sell the pictures to the *Daily Mail* so Suzy will be pleased.

Monday 25
Fat Kylie has not sold the pictures to the *Daily Mail*. Brady deleted them by mistake trying to take a photo of his

bottom. I declined to see the picture. Scarlet says Hugo Thorndyke's political career is over anyway. Margot Gyp, who is the Ladies' Captain at the Golf Club, saw the fight and she is the most influential woman in a twenty-mile radius.

Tuesday 26

Mr Wilmott has found out about the election betting. He has banned gambling from school premises. Ms Hopwood-White looked worried. She has £5 on Ali Hassan.

Wednesday 27

A lot of post arrived for Grandpa, thanking him for supporting Charles Kennedy, Michael Howard, George Galloway, and Robert Kilroy-Silk. He is livid as he has never been a member of any organization in his life, not even the RSPB, on the grounds they might fritter his money on pigeons, which he does not approve of and which are honorary rats anyway. Mum looked at the letters. One of them said, 'Thank you for your interesting suggestion of using "Evergreen" by Will Young as a theme tune.' James has been banned from political activity until he is eighteen. Mum is going to buy a shredder from WHSmith this morning to prevent further identity theft.

6 p.m.
Mum has shredded the entire contents of Dad's filing cabinet plus a letter from Granny Clegg to the dog. What is anyone going to do with that?

8 p.m.
Mum has agreed not to shred anything of Dad's before he has rubber-stamped it. In her enthusiasm she shredded the pin number to Dad's new credit card, before he had memorized it. James said it was 8187.

Thursday 28
Suzy is threatening to take the *Walden Chronicle* to the Press Complaints Commission. Their lead story was the new bollards on the High Street—love them or hate them? There was no mention of the St George's Day Parade gang fight. She has accused the editor, Deirdre Roberts, of running a media cover-up because Deirdre's cousin is married to Hugo Thorndyke's sister. She said that Saffron Walden is like Baghdad and the Thorndykes are the Husseins, with fingers in every pie and spies on every corner. Personally, I think this is stretching it a bit far.

Friday 29
Scarlet has done a terrible thing. She let one of the senior goths pierce her nose with a pair of compasses in the

lower school toilets at first break. It is lucky they did it in there because she was sick almost immediately because of the blood. The goths had to call for the school nurse (aka Mrs Leech, the school secretary) to administer revival techniques. Mrs Leech just wafted her with a maths text book and told someone to get a Coke out of the machine to boost her blood sugar. I hope that is not what Tony Blair is training all his extra nurses to do.

Scarlet revived after the Coke and a Galaxy Ripple. She said it was a rite of passage for the goths to be pierced in as many places as possible. I assume she means body parts, rather than various toilets. Suzy is going to go mad. This could be another major setback in her election campaign.

Saturday 30

Suzy has ordered Scarlet to put a plaster over the stud because she has an important public appearance at the Town Hall tonight. It is going to be like *Question Time* on telly, with Deirdre Roberts as David Dimbleby. Scarlet, Sad Ed, and I are going to watch.

8 p.m.

Things did not go according to plan. Suzy has revealed herself to be a former drug taker and sexual deviant. Everything was going OK after the first few questions ('What is your favourite Saffron Walden landmark?'

'Should so-called graffiti "artists" be locked up?' and 'Is France our friend or foe?'). Then Deirdre asked the panel if they had ever taken drugs. Suzy said, 'Yes, and yes I did inhale, does that make me a criminal?' Deirdre said that yes, actually, it did. Suzy should have known better. Deirdre thinks speeding should carry a minimum of life. The next question was about the bollards, but Suzy got an emergency counselling case on her mobile. So, when Deirdre got to Suzy's answer, all everyone could hear was Suzy shouting, 'Dennis, I really think you should consider using more lubricant.' Deirdre looked as if she was going to faint and Hugo Thorndyke seized his opportunity and took over the microphone. He said that Saffron Walden should send a message to Tony Blair that normal middle-class law-abiding citizens won't tolerate this kind of perversion. Margot Gyp, the influential Ladies' Golf Captain, said, 'Hear, hear.' Sad Ed said it was the sound of the fat lady singing. He is trying to be poetic in everyday situations.

Sunday 1

Rogation Sunday

Looked rogation up in the dictionary. It said supplication. So I looked that up. It is something about thanking the gods for victory. I suspect Hugo Thorndyke is doing that right now.

Treena came for her conjugal visit. She looked very pale and worried. She and Grandpa went for a Benson and Hedges in the garden. I heard her say, 'December, Ern. What are we going to do? All the sick and the shitting everywhere.' Her husband, Des, must be a heroin addict. I have seen it on TV. She is going to help him go cold turkey when he gets out in December. When Grandpa came back in he looked pale as well. I'm not surprised. I've seen a photo of Des and he has a tattoo on his neck and wears a Burberry baseball cap. I don't think they did any conjugating today.

Scarlet is out at CHURCH! Suzy is trying to revamp her image after yesterday's disaster. I don't think Scarlet is going to sway any old ladies with her pierced nose, though. It has blown up and gone septic. She looks like Shrek.

Monday 2

May Day Holiday (UK)

Yet another tedious provincial bank holiday. Went over to Sad Ed's but he was feigning illness under threat of being taken to an Aled Jones Fan Club (Essex branch) meeting in Harlow. I asked what he was pretending to have and he said scurvy. Mr and Mrs Thomas are easily duped. Mrs Thomas had gone to Mr Patel's for emergency orange juice.

Took the dog out for a walk into town. Something odd happened. We saw Grandpa and Treena coming out of the emergency chemist's and I am sure Grandpa saw us but he hurried Treena over the road into the White Horse pub instead. The dog tried to follow and wanted to wait outside until he came out. But Fat Kylie was also out there with Paris-Marie and Brady, waiting for their mum and I didn't want people to think I was related so I went to Mr Patel's and bought some Gypsy Creams and we ate them at home while we watched *Chitty Chitty Bang Bang*. I do not think that film should be shown before the watershed. I had to close my eyes on several occasions and the dog whimpered throughout the whole of the child catcher scene. I think it brought back memories of Mrs Peason.

· ·

Tuesday 3

Scarlet's nose is horrendous. It is actually seeping green stuff now. Ms Hopwood-White demanded that she remove the nose stud but Scarlet refused on the grounds that it was regulation gold. Ms Hopwood-White pointed out that the rule referred to single ear piercings only but Scarlet said she was being body-partist and possibly anti-Hindu. So Ms Hopwood-White sent her to Mrs Leech to get some Savlon.

Wednesday 4

The nose stud is out. Suzy said the deformity could cost her the election, plus Scarlet got mild septicaemia and went all shaky during *BBC Breakfast*. Bob had to take her to work to get it treated so she missed PE this morning (hockey—result 27–2 to Fat Kylie's menacing team, plus two minor electrifications). When she came back she had a bandage across her face like Britney after her nose job. Thin Kylie was instantly impressed. She is already planning extensive surgery. Her mum has saved her child benefit since she was two so she can get a boob job. I said I didn't think that was what the government had hoped she would spend it on. Kylie said what could be more beneficial than a career-boosting DD cup, look at Jordan? Scarlet says she is going to get the nose stud done properly at Camden Market as soon as it is healed. That is like a goth pilgrimage site.

Thursday 5

Ascension Day
Election Day
8 a.m.
Grandpa is refusing to vote. He says no one has offered him anything worth leaving his *Daily Mail* and bowl of

Grape-Nuts for. I said, 'But the political future of Saffron Walden hangs in the balance.' Dad said, 'Yes, between a drug-addled nymphomaniac and a pensioner-beating madman.' James offered to use his vote for him, but Mum shredded the voting card before he could try.

10 a.m.
The John Major High polling station (i.e. a cardboard box outside the lower school canteen) is a hive of political activity (i.e. handing out free things). Ali Hassan has Michael Howard protractors, Pippa has badges with a pop star of your choice (using her sister's badge machine and a pile of *Heat* magazines), Oona Rickets has Stop the War organic lesbian-made flapjacks and, shamefully, Jack, Justin, and Sophie Jacobs are handing out Microwave Muffins (cooked in the sixth form common room microwave, which is ten years old and is under investigation for leaking radiation by the science club). The maths club are running exit polls. They say it is too close to call but that a change from blueberry to double chocolate could swing it for Jack.

3 p.m.
Jack has won the election! He has a majority of thirty-one. Pippa Newbold came second and Ali Hassan and Oona Rickets joint third with twenty-seven votes each. Oona claims she got at least thirty but that several Criminals and Retards spoiled their ballot papers. I lurked near Justin hoping that the post-election madness would rub off on

him and he would throw me against the Coke machine and kiss me passionately, but he was too busy fending Year Seven girls off Jack.

This is all a good omen for Suzy though. I predict she will beat Hugo Thorndyke and join Tony Blair's babes in the Houses of Parliament tomorrow.

2 a.m.
Scarlet rang. Suzy did not win. She says the tweed Saddam Hussein got in. I assume she meant Hugo Thorndyke but Mum came down in her Marks & Spencer's dressing gown and told Scarlet not to ring at such an ungodly hour and then put the phone down.

Friday 6
Scarlet says Suzy has taken to her bed. She is playing Sheryl Crow albums and compulsively eating sesame snaps. Bob wants her to stick to sex instead of politics.

Jack says it is the last time he enters a political contest as well. He says there can be no victory in leading an electorate who are swayed by convenience cake. He is not leading an electorate anyway. Ms Hopwood-White failed to secure permission from Mr Wilmott to grant the winner any powers so he is a straw doll (I learnt that from Jeremy Paxman).

Granny and Grandpa Clegg rang in a panic. They are thinking of moving because a Lib Dem got in in St

Slaughter. Mum went pale and warned them that the Lib Dems were strong in Saffron Walden but Granny Clegg said they would rather move to Wales than Saffron Walden and anyway they were thinking more of Camborne, which is Conservative, bordering on BNP. Mum looked relieved. Then Granny Clegg said she and Grandpa wanted to come up and exercise their dog visiting rights in a fortnight and Mum looked weary again.

Saturday 7

I am glad the election is over. Now I can concentrate on more pressing matters. Like, where is my period? Scarlet got hers over a year ago. She is already using organic tampons. She says Miss Vicar told the ski-trip girls that cold weather could bring it on. Why are we having a clement spell? This is typical. I am going to have to wait until November or pray for an unseasonal snowstorm. I have looked it up on the internet. There is even a name for sad people like me. Apparently the two main causes are anorexia or genetic inheritance. I don't think six hours of anorexia count so it must be Mum's fault. It suggests that I ask her when she got her period. Gross. I expect Granny Clegg banned periods in St Slaughter anyway. They probably still call it the 'curse'. I will suffer in silence like Joan of Arc.

Sunday 8

Treena came over for lunch again. I don't think she likes lemon meringue pie. She went all pale when she saw it and ran out and threw up in the downstairs loo. Mum was annoyed. She sees it as a waste of food. I don't know why. It comes out at some point.

At least she has given up smoking though. Mum asked her why she had finally come to her senses and she said, 'It weren't my flaming idea. It's those bloody doctors.' But when Grandpa went out for a Benson and Hedges I noticed she stood in the cloud of fumes, passively inhaling furiously.

Mum says the sooner smoking is banned the better. She says it is anti-social behaviour. She is thinking of starting a catalogue of anti-social incidents in the area. It will be enormous. She thinks Clive and Marjory should get an ASBO for owning a caravan.

Monday 9

We are having a sex talk at school on Wednesday. Ms Hopwood-White gave us all a note to get permission from our parents. Scarlet says Suzy won't let her go. I said I thought Suzy would be all for it but Scarlet says Suzy is of the opinion that the school sex education curriculum is outdated and could set her back years. I am going. I do not have the advantage of a liberated mother or a library full of sex manuals. Sad Ed is going to forge his mum's signature. She still thinks Aled Jones is a virgin.

• •

Tuesday 10

Everyone has gone sex talk mad. Sad Ed says that at his cousins' school in Leighton Buzzard everyone put anonymous questions in a hat and the 'sexpert' person answered all of them, even whether you should take out your braces when you give a blow job. Mark Lambert said, 'You don't wear braces, fat boy, so you'll be all right.' So Ms Hopwood-White sent him to Mr Wilmott. I don't think he and Kylie should be allowed to come to the talk—they have an unfair advantage. Scarlet says we are all going to be disappointed.

• •

Wednesday 11

Scarlet was right. I might as well have sat in the library with her, Ali Hassan, and the Jehovah's Witness children. There was no sexpert. It was Miss Beadle and a plastic penis model. I think Mr Wilmott should have chosen a more appropriate teacher. Everyone knows she has no experience with male genitalia. There were no free condoms and no questions about blow jobs. Sad Ed was visibly disappointed.

A mattress has been dumped outside Clive and Marjory's. It appeared overnight. Marjory says it is the

114

O'Grady brothers. They have been running a black market waste collection and disposal firm. Mum is beside herself with potential ASBO excitement. She has catalogued the mattress in a WHSmith notebook and is going to write to the council. (Marjory has palsy in her right hand from excess Jenga playing.)

Thursday 12

The mattress is still there. The dog has taken to sitting on it. Grandpa says he is thinking of joining him. He says it gets the sun most of the day and Mum can't tell him off for spilling Hobnob crumbs.

Friday 13

I hate Friday the thirteenth. Every time anything odd happens at school everyone says, 'Ooooh, Friday the thirteenth!' in a stupid voice. At first break Tracey Hughes dropped her Mars bar and it landed end up on the piece of gum she had just spat out. She might as well have twisted her head around 360 degrees by the reaction from the three Year Eights who saw it happen. They watch too much *Most Haunted*.

Scarlet is celebrating though. It must be some sort of goth festival day. She has got out *Scream 3* and *I Still Know What You Did Last Summer* to watch later. Sad Ed says they are Hollywood trash and that we should watch the

Wicker Man or *The Exorcist* if we want to watch real horror.

10.30 p.m.
Have just got back from Scarlet's. I am never watching horror films again. Even Sad Ed got scared and had to hold my hand. I notice he did not hold Scarlet's hand though. Maybe the studded glove put him off. Scarlet made Bob bring us home in case evil forces were lurking in Waitrose car park. Bob accidentally drove over the mattress when he was reversing up Clive and Marjory's drive to turn around. One of the springs got caught in the undercarriage of the Volvo and the mattress is now stuck on Marjory's flower bed. Bob drove off quickly before anyone could see.

Saturday 14
Marjory is all het up. She claims mysterious Friday the thirteenth forces have moved the mattress. She has asked Mum if she thinks an exorcism is necessary. Mum gave her a glass of cooking sherry and said it was probably just anti-social council estate children or cats. I did not tell her that it was a thirty-nine-year-old gynaecologist in a sick-smelling Volvo. It would have ruined her image of today's youth. How could cats move a mattress anyway? They are not co-ordinated enough. Mum has catalogued it under subsection A of the mattress misdemeanour.

Sunday 15

Whit Sunday

9 a.m.

Barry the Blade is asleep on the mattress. Mum has called 999 but the police said that sleeping vagrants were not an emergency, beard or no beard. Mum said that he was a known knife fetishist and might have progressed to guns but the policeman laughed and said, 'This isn't Hackney, love.' How right he is. Mum said he will be laughing on the other side of his face when he is mopping up blood on Summerdale Road. I think Barry the Blade looks peaceful though.

11 a.m.

Grandpa has been sent to his room. He made Barry the Blade a cup of tea and took him out two Duchy Originals. I'm not sure if Mum is more angry about Barry the Blade or the biscuits.

Am going over to Scarlet's for ritual TV viewing. I hope Barry the Blade is still there when I get back. He is the most interesting thing to happen to our road since the legendary gnome stand-off at Number 38. Maybe he is not a mad murderer after all but a misunderstood philosopher type who has fallen on hard times, like Stephen Hawking but without the keyboard and wheelchair. Maybe he is out there thinking about the space-time continuum. I could engage him in philosophical discussions and discover his genius and then I could be his muse. I told Scarlet on the phone and she said the mattress could be a live art installation. Apparently, Suzy once went to look at some ginger actress asleep in a box. We could become millionaires for our mattress art, especially with a philosophical tramp sleeping on it.

4 p.m.
Barry the Blade has gone. Clearly he wasn't having philosophical thoughts. He started singing 'I'm Just a Love Machine' so Marjory hosed him down on the pretence of watering the tulips. I told Mum about the live art installation and phoning the Tate Gallery but she said the only people she was phoning were the council first thing in the morning.

Monday 16
Mum has called the Uttlesford environmental health department re. the escalating mattress situation. They have not agreed to remove it but are sending someone out to inspect it and assess its position. Apparently, if the majority of the mattress is on Clive and Marjory's garden then they will have to dispose of it themselves. Mum measured it. It is fifty-six centimetres on Marjory's poo-smeared tulips and seventy-two centimetres on the council-owned pavement. She is triumphant.

Tuesday 17

The man from the council came and looked at the mattress after school. He says it is definitely a menace but that he can't get it moved until at least next Monday. Mum threatened to call the *Walden Chronicle* and he said he could probably fit it in tomorrow. Mum rang the *Walden Chronicle* anyway. Her anti-social behaviour crusade knows no bounds.

Wednesday 18

The mattress is gone. The dustbin men took it away. Mum asked if they were going to check it for forensic evidence. They said no, they were going to take it to a junk shop in Cambridge. Apparently students will pay good money for a second-hand mattress. Even one covered in Hobnobs and dog hair.

Thursday 19

The mattress has made the *Walden Chronicle* under the headline 'Dumped Mattress Madness'.

Mum has rung the paper to complain. She says the piece makes her sound like she is the anti-social one. She is never satisfied.

Personally I think a mattress is an ideal object to trip up on, providing an instant crash mat to break the fall.

DUMPED MATTRESS MADNESS

A mattress left abandoned for literally a week has finally been removed following pressure from anti-social campaigner, Janet Riley. Mrs Riley, 40, said the mattress had become a health, crime, and environmental hazard. 'It could have seriously hurt someone if they had tripped on it, not to mention the potential of it being set on fire by thugs.'

Friday 20

Granny Clegg rang to make arrangements for their dog access visit. Auntie Joyless is going to get her 'hooge' verrucas prayed off at a church convention in Newmarket, so she is going to drop her and Grandpa on the M11 at 9 a.m., traffic and foot pain pending. Granny wants Dad to pick them up from the Junction 8 services and to bring 'Valerie' with him. She says they want some time with it alone, out of the brainwashing grip of Grandpa Riley. Grandpa Riley says he is going to train the dog to attack anyone who thinks 'hooge' is a word.

I can tell Mum is dreading the weekend. She has hoovered the stairs three times and cleaned out the cupboard under the sink. At least she doesn't have to share a room with James.

. . . .

Saturday 21
9.30 a.m.
Junction 8 services. There is no sign of Granny and Grandpa Clegg so we are eating proscribed Egg McMuffins. Dad says it is payback for making him wait around a motorway service station when he could be at home reading the motoring section of the *Telegraph*.

10 a.m.
Dad has phoned Mum but it is engaged. It is probably Auntie Joyless from a payphone on the A30 saying they have diverted to Trago Mills.

11.45 a.m.
Still no sign of Granny and Grandpa Clegg. Phone is still engaged at home.
Motorway services are a hotbed of adulterous sex. I have seen at least three suspicious couples running into the Travelodge next door and then coming out an hour later, including Tracey Hughes's mum and one of the traffic police. I will not blab though. Tracey Hughes's mum is hard as nails.

121

2 p.m.
No sign. Have eaten a Little Chef omelette and a chocolate ice cream sundae. The dog has eaten four bags of Doritos and an Early Starter Breakfast.

2.15 p.m.
Dad finally got through to Mum. Apparently James has been online all morning learning about Middle Earth. Dad said that was a good argument for broadband but Mum said she was not going to fork out an extra £7.99 a month to encourage an eight year old's Tolkien habit. Then she told Dad to widen his search. Dad said he was not going to cruise up and down the motorway looking for a pair of yokels. Mum then said something severe because we are back in the car heading towards London.

5 p.m.
We have been to every service station on the M11. No one has seen two short pensioners with odd accents carrying Spar bags. We thought we had struck lucky at Junction 3 but it turned out to be two Romanian panel beaters. Dad says he is going home.

5 p.m.
Granny and Grandpa Clegg were already at home. They arrived in a police car fifteen minutes ago. Auntie Joyless got confused and dropped them at the Q8 Garage in

Stansted. Mum asked why they hadn't rung and Granny Clegg said she had, but it had been engaged. (James has been sent to his room and internet access has been reduced to half an hour, off peak only.) Apparently they walked all the way from Stansted but got lost and scared near the Whiteshot Estate when a 'darkie' (possibly Mrs Wong or one of the Hassans) tried to help them so they called 999 again.

They were overjoyed to see 'Valerie'. But the dog got excited at the smell of Fray Bentos and immediately threw up its Doritos and Early Starter Breakfast. Grandpa Riley said he felt like joining it. So Mum sent him to his room.

I said it was all a lesson in the importance of mobile phones. Which was when I got sent to join James. Mum is just annoyed because Clive and Marjory saw the police car and now probably think she is harbouring criminals.

I do not hold out much hope for tomorrow. Treena is coming for tea. They are not likely to see eye to eye.

Sunday 22

Trinity Sunday

Woke up with a giant Des Lynam lying next to me and the dog drooling on my face. I don't know how James gets any sleep, the dog has to be let out to wee at least twice in the night.

123

The day got progressively worse from there. Granny and Grandpa Clegg wanted to take Valerie for a walk but Grandpa Riley said they couldn't be trusted on their own not to steal him or teach him Cornish gibberish so he made me follow them round Saffron Walden. I hid several paces behind with my hood up. When we got back, Treena's Datsun was on the drive and she was snogging Grandpa in the back seat. Granny Clegg said, 'Shut your eyes, Norman,' and Grandpa Riley wound the window down and said, 'You're just jealous, Joan,' so Grandpa Clegg told him to get out of the car and say it, so he did, but luckily Mum came out and said lunch was ready.

No one spoke during lunch. It was punctuated only by the sound of Treena throwing up in the downstairs loo.

Then, Auntie Joyless arrived early from Newmarket. She makes Mum look permissive. Her lips are so thin they are non-existent and she wears men's shoes. She asked if I had got to Corinthians 3, Chapter 4 yet. I said I had yet to enjoy that part (or any part). I asked about her veruccas and she said they were definitely smaller, thanks to the power of Reverend Billy's prayer. Grandpa Riley said that Reverend Billy sounded like a charlatan and that a good dose of Bazuka would work wonders. James asked if Auntie Joyless had checked Reverend Billy's ecclesiastical credentials. Auntie Joyless said that God didn't need to hand out identification cards and that Reverend Billy had cured Barbara Pengelly's women's troubles and that was good enough for her. Then Treena came out of the bathroom after being sick again and said, 'Christ on a bike, I'll be throwing up my arse if this goes on.' Auntie Joyless snapped 'Blasphemer' at her. Grandpa Riley said how dare she shout at someone in Treena's condition. I said 'What condition?' but no one heard me. Mum said it might be a good idea if Treena went out for a little while but Grandpa Riley said it was 'pissing down' and she wasn't to know Auntie Joyless was a god botherer. Which would have been bad enough, except that he actually called her 'Joyless'. Auntie Joyless stormed out to the Mini Metro and said it was the last time she was leaving Cornwall, verrucas or no verrucas. Granny Clegg said, 'Get the Spar bags, Norman, we're going home.' Grandpa Clegg said something unrepeatable about Grandpa Riley and Auntie Joyless said she would pray for us all. Then the dog saw that Granny Clegg was leaving and made a run for the Mini Metro but Auntie Joyless slammed the door and the dog hit the side panel making a huge dog-shaped dent and knocking off the wing mirror. Granny Clegg screamed 'Valerie!' but Auntie Joyless drove off quickly before she could get out.

Mum says she is banning Treena and ending dog visiting rights. Dad says it shows why Rover have gone out of business if a dog can cause that much damage.

I think Treena is bulimic. It is very Jacqueline Wilson. I will try to get on her side and help her overcome her awful 'condition'.

Monday 23

There is no justice in the world. Thin Kylie has won the lottery. She was not in school to share the joyous news, she is on a celebratory week at Disneyworld, but, according to Fat Kylie, her stepdad Terry got a million on the lottery on Saturday. Why don't we do the lottery? Actually, I know why and that is because Mum says there's more chance of being killed by a donkey and she would rather put the £1 into her Barclays Saver Account. Where is the fun in that? If I won, I would buy a mansion in Derbyshire like Mr Darcy's where I could languish about looking tragic and give the rest to poor people.

Mark Lambert is dead excited. He reckons he is going to get a minibike and a season ticket to West Ham. Scarlet says he is an idiot and that Kylie will dump him the minute she gets back. She can afford to now. The money will move her up a social circle, like Heather Mills McCartney. She will be able to buy real Burberry instead of the Made in Taiwan stuff off the Saturday market.

To add insult to injury, I have a dentist's appointment tomorrow with sadistic Mrs Wong. I have tried to change dentist several times (every six months, in fact) but the only other dentist with space was Mr Webb, who is a renowned drunk and once tried to snog Leanne Jones, according to Leanne. So Mum won't let me see him. I would rather run the gauntlet of a drunken child molester than Mrs Wong. She is evil personified. I may well write to Hugo Thorndyke MP to complain about the general lack of suitable dentists.

Tuesday 24

I cannot speak. One side of my face is swollen and I keep drooling down my chin. Mrs Wong gave me two fillings. I asked if I could have a second opinion but she pointed her drill at me and said, 'Don't be silly, little girl. You want more pain when teeth go black and drop out then I have to give you crown?' I did not want to argue with a madwoman with what looked like a Black and Decker, so I let her give me two injections and then lecture me on the perils of the western diet and why all my teeth will fall out by the time I'm forty if I don't give up Coke. Clearly she has not seen the relationship her son Alan has with the school vending machine. He has been known to eat three Mars bars in one break. Luckily I was so disabled I could not go back to school. I am on the sofa with a tea towel to catch the dribble (Mum's idea) watching *Bargain Hunt*. That man's hair is unfeasibly large.

Sad Ed came round in the evening. He is devastated. Mrs Noakes from WHSmith (no chin; bad perm; calls trousers 'slacks') rang his mum to tell her that he had bought a copy of *Lady Chatterley's Lover* in his lunch break. She is concerned that he bought it for the sex parts not the literary merit (she is right). He has had his pocket money stopped and his bookshelves checked for further potentially damaging material. *Romeo and Juliet*, *The Sleepover Club*, and *You and Your Body* (pop-up version) have been confiscated pending closer inspection. He says it is like *Fahrenheit 451* in his house, even Enid Blyton is under suspicion. I'm not sure what he means. But it is very hot in there. Mr Thomas always has the heating on full because of his bonsai collection.

Wednesday 25

School is still awash with lottery madness. I hope Mrs Britcher did not tick the 'no publicity' box on the ticket because, according to Fat Kylie, the *Walden Chronicle* is camped out on their doorstep awaiting their return. Tracey Hughes told her mum who told the police who told the fat traffic warden who told his wife who is the receptionist at the paper. Nothing is secret in this town. How I long for the anonymity of London, where the newsagent is not likely to inform on you for buying a sex book and your neighbours are more likely to be drug dealing terrorists than Jenga-playing accountants.

Thursday 26

Thin Kylie's mum, Cherie, is on the front page of the *Walden Chronicle*. It is a picture of her dressed as Britney Spears in last year's carnival looky-likey competition (she came second after Les Brewster as a bald John Prescott) and the headline 'She's So Lucky'. (I think the reference to Britney's minor hit will be lost. They should have put 'Toxic'.) The *Walden Chronicle*, in a never-before-seen act of investigative journalism, managed to trace the Britchers to Disneyworld (Mark Lambert told them Kylie's mobile number) and interviewed Cherie at the poolside bar. I think she may have been drunk at the time because a lot of the words had asterisks in the middle.

Mum said it was proof there was no God and that they will only spend it on gold taps and Austrian blinds. James said that, statistically, most lottery winners spend their money on holidays and cars and that he hoped that Auntie Joyless did not know she felt like that about our good Lord. Mum did not look pleased at his cavernous knowledge or new-found religious leanings. I think she is rueing the day she bought *Encyclopaedia Britannica* on CD-Rom and sent him to a primary school with a vicar as the headmaster.

Friday 27

Thank God it is half term next week. I do not want to see Kylie or hear about her again. Everyone is mad with anticipation for her return, even Melanie Bazley in Year

Eight whom she beat up last week for getting the last Double Decker out of the Coke and crisp machine (note correct use of whom, as learnt in double English today before it got suspended when Mark Lambert tried to belch 'Whole Again' and was sick by mistake).

I am all alone for a week as well. Sad Ed is going to Butlin's in Minehead and Scarlet is going on a tantric sex retreat in India with Bob and Suzy to help her recover from the election disappointment. (Scarlet is not going to do anything tantric, she is going to commune with indigenous cultures.) I asked Mum if we could go on holiday and she said we were, in August, as usual. I said that Granny Clegg's was hardly a new experience and she said there was nothing India had that Cornwall didn't. I said exotic wildlife and curry and she said, 'Looe Monkey Sanctuary and the Rajpoot in Truro.' I will never get to Paris at this rate.

Saturday 28

Grandpa has broken up with Treena. I asked if it was to do with the throwing up and he said 'kind of'. I am not surprised. It is very offputting. She was sick seven times last Sunday, beating the dog's record. It is very disappointing from a tragic and interesting point of view. Mum is relieved though. I think the whole thing was jeopardizing her reputation as a law-abiding puritan.

Sunday 29

Grandpa is moping round the house. I asked if he wanted to watch *The O.C.* with me (Mum had taken James to the museum with Mumtaz to look at its vast collection of old coins and a stuffed lion). But he said all the age-gap relationships reminded him of himself and Treena so he turned it off. He is deluded. No one on *The O.C.* would wear nylon for starters. Or say 'bag of shite'.

Monday 30

Spring Bank Holiday (UK)

No school and no friends. I am going to devote this week to bettering myself through literature. I am going to read *Emma*. Which is apparently just like *Clueless* but set in England.

5 p.m.

It is not like *Clueless*. There is too much fainting. And the men sound awful. But it is good for me. So I am going to persevere.

Tuesday 31

Mum's WHSmith ASBO catalogue is out again. There is a dodgy man with tattoos loitering with intent outside the For Sale house over the road. It has been empty for months since Mr and Mrs Lawson got divorced and moved to Haverhill and Benidorm respectively. James says it is overpriced for a four-bed semi with a through lounge, but it does have the advantage of a south-facing garden.

10 a.m.
Mum has called 999. The man has gone through the side gate and has not been seen for seven minutes.

11 a.m.
It was not a burglar. It was a prospective buyer. Apparently he got tired of waiting for the estate agent and was just having a look through the patio doors to see whether his L-shaped sofa could fit it. Mum said L-shaped sofas were a crime in themselves. She is annoyed because the police declined her offer to see her ASBO catalogue. It is now several pages long.

Wednesday 1

Grandpa is missing Treena. I caught him sniffing an old cigarette packet earlier and his daytime TV viewing has gone through the roof because he is refusing to go to the Twilight Years Day Centre in case she is working. I hope they get back together soon. I cannot watch *Neighbours* twice in one day.

Also, I have given up on *Emma*. It is totally implausible and not very tragic. Am reading Dad's *Da Vinci Code* instead. It is set in Paris so is bound to be good.

Thursday 2

That tattooed man must have bought the house opposite. The For Sale sign has come down. Mum says she thinks he is a cash buyer—probably a gangster from East London spending his ill-gotten gains. I hope so, he might have Ray Winstone or Guy and Madonna round to dinner. Or he might have a glamorous gangster daughter my age, which would be excellent. There is nothing to do round here when Scarlet and Sad Ed are away.

Grandpa has caved in and called Treena. Even he couldn't cope with that many makeover programmes. He is going to see her on Sunday. They are meeting on neutral territory (the White Horse). He says he is willing to meet her demands, whatever the consequences. What is she demanding? More food?

Friday 3

Our new neighbours have moved in. They are not gangsters from East London, they are Kylie Britcher and her lottery-winning mum and stepdad! James and I watched in horror from my window as the removal men carried in a flab-buster machine, a tropical-themed drinks cabinet, and a four-poster bed with leopard-print canopy.

James says it is the beginning of the end of Summerdale Road. He is right.

7 p.m.

Cherie just came over to invite us for cocktails and karaoke tomorrow to 'celebrate' her and Terry's arrival! She has invited Clive and Marjory as well but they said they had a regional Jenga bout in Bishop's Stortford. Mum was too slow trying to think of an excuse so we are going to have to go. Kylie is going to go mental when she knows I live here.

Saturday 4

Sad Ed rang and asked me to go over to commiserate over his week of hell at Butlin's (i.e. group activity and swimming, revealing flabby upper arms). Told Ed about Kylie and he agreed it was a life-threatening situation. He said I can stay at his if I want. But his spare room is taken over by his mum's Aled Jones memorabilia collection, and last time I stayed I got the feeling Aled was watching me sleep, so I said I would take my chances.

James has got out of going because he is only eight and Mum does not want him exposed to karaoke or too many E-numbers. Mum made Grandpa promise to put him to bed at 8.30 and not to let him watch anything on ITV. There is no hope. Grandpa is addicted to *You've Been Framed*.

11 p.m.
I should have gone to Ed's. Even a night with forty-seven Aled Joneses would have been better than that. The Britcher's house is Mum's Room 101. Their doorbell plays 'Rule Britannia' and they have Alsatian dog statues guarding the porch. Cherie came to the door wearing a figure-hugging halter top and miniskirt. It was in stark contrast to Mum who was in figure-concealing beige Marks & Spencer's linen and Clark's sandals. At first I thought I had had a lucky escape because Kylie was nowhere to be seen, but Cherie said she was in her room playing Nintendo and I should go and join her. I looked to Mum to get me out of it, but she was too busy staring in horror at the Austrian blinds so I had to go upstairs.

Kylie was on the phone, presumably to Mark Lambert. She said, 'F**k off, I ain't telling you . . . no, I ain't . . . no I ain't . . . oh, all right, Wonderbra and a thong . . . the black one from BHS.' Then she saw me and said 'Oh . . . my . . . God. There is, like, a retard in my room. Laters.'

Then she looked at me menacingly and said, 'What . . . the f**k . . . are you doing in 'ere?'

I explained the proximity of our houses, now that her family had had the good fortune to win the lottery, and she said, 'Don't tell me that fat poof friend of yours lives near here as well. This is, like, sadland central.'

I told her that indeed Sad Ed did live two hundred yards away on the corner of Loompits Avenue, but that he was neither fat nor gay. And she said, 'Are you, like, blind?'

I suggested we should go downstairs and do the karaoke and ignore our differences but she said, 'Yeah, right. I'm going down Barry Island in half an hour to see Mark, I ain't singing no Amarillo shite.'

I said wouldn't her mum mind (Barry Island is the car park on the Common where the O'Gradys and similar youths go to rev up their Fiestas and have sex) but she said, 'She'll be pissed in half an hour and forget I'm in anyway.'

At that point I left and went downstairs to find Dad singing 'Is This The Way To Amarillo?' and Mum sipping Appletise with an umbrella in it. Cherie cheered when Dad finished and put her hand on his arm. I noticed Dad did not try to remove it. He is easily swayed by tight clothes.

Then Cherie said, 'It's *Grease* next, who wants to do that?'

So before she could make me sing 'You're the One That I Want' with Terry I said I would go home and check on James and Grandpa.

Cherie said, 'Oh, I didn't know you had two, Jan. How old is he?'

Mum went all tight-lipped (name shortening is one of her banned activities) and said he was eight. Cherie said, 'Oh, an accident. One was enough for me, all that sweating and heaving and pain. It's not natural, is it?'

And Terry said, 'And that was just the conception!'

Dad laughed and Mum shot him one of her looks so he pretended to have a coughing fit instead.

Cherie said, 'Not like now. When our girls get pregnant they can book 'emselves in for the slice and they get a tummy tuck at the same time. I've got stretch marks the size of dinner plates right down to my hoo-ha.'

Mum said she didn't think I was planning on pregnancy any time soon and Cherie said, 'But you can't stop their urges, can you, Jan. They're all at it.'

Luckily, before Mum could highlight my lack of experience at even snogging anyone, James arrived to say that Grandpa and Treena were in the bath with a box of Celebrations (Treena showed up unannounced—apparently she couldn't wait until tomorrow to see Grandpa's grisly bits) so he couldn't do a poo (downstairs toilet blocked again). Mum said she had better sort Grandpa out so that James could poo in peace. But Dad, who had just been handed a pint glass of Bailey's and what looked like fruit salad, said he would stay.

I don't know exactly what happened after that, but Treena has gone home, Grandpa is on a caution for attempting conjugation outside previously agreed terms and conditions, and Dad is asleep on the sofa.

Thank God Scarlet is back from Bob and Suzy's tantric sex retreat tomorrow. My life on Summerdale Road has become fraught with danger.

. . . .

Sunday 5

Went round to Scarlet's with Sad Ed to hear about the tantric sex week. Suzy is definitely back to normal. She came downstairs in a kaftan looking red and sweaty and said, 'Oh, Rachel, my beautiful child, you must go to India, it is so liberating.' Then she danced back into the bedroom where I could clearly see Bob naked on the floor reading a sex manual. Scarlet says they have been at it for forty-seven hours now, including on the flight from Mumbai.

Ed says he saw a programme about tantric sex once on Discovery Home and Leisure. He says it sounded painful and boring to him. Scarlet said she wouldn't know, she spent all her time lying on her mat in the hut and reading Kafka. I said I thought she was going to commune with indigenous cultures. She said she went outside once but she passed out because her goth clothes were too black and heavy in the heat.

Got home and the two Kylies were sat on the front wall drinking Shandy Bass. I have catalogued them in Mum's ASBO book for underage drinking and loitering. Treena was in Grandpa's bedroom, conjugating again.

I have a mind to catalogue them as well. It is highly anti-social to have sex when everyone else is trying to watch *Antiques Roadshow*.

Monday 6

There has been a stand-off at school over the seating arrangements in the lower school canteen. It is over the free school dinners table. Mrs Brain makes all the poor people, like the Kylies, Ali Hassan, and the rest of the Whiteshot Estate, sit on one table so she can monitor who doesn't have to pay. But now that Thin Kylie is rich she has been ejected and has to sit with normal people instead. Fat Kylie is up in arms. She was used to getting all Thin Kylie's leftovers.

Sad Ed said it was like South Africa before they banned apartheid and accused Mr Wilmott of being a white supremacist. So Mr Wilmott gave Sad Ed detention but Scarlet told Mr Wilmott that he was as good as holding him political prisoner and that she was texting Suzy immediately for Labour Party back-up. Mr Wilmott panicked and agreed to end the 'povvy table' but Mrs Brain went mad and said it would be a free-for-all with the free meal tokens (this is after Stacey O'Grady forged two hundred last year and no one paid for food for two days). So now there is going to be a discussion at next week's PTA meeting.

Scarlet has diverted her hummus sandwich rally to an anti-class-segregation one. She says she will not rest until the Kylies can sit where they like to eat their chips and processed meat products.

. . . .

Tuesday 7

I am finally getting to go to Paris! There is a school trip at the end of the month for anyone doing French GCSE. Ms Hopwood-White is jubilant—she had to get Mr Wilmott to lift his ban on school outings, imposed after last year's Year Ten Geography field trip to Wales when Darren Woodley accidentally set fire to the youth hostel trying to light his farts. Me and Sad Ed are going but Scarlet says she will be at Glastonbury with Bob and Suzy. (I asked Mum if I could go to Glastonbury last year but she said it was a hotbed of illegality and potentially eardrum-damaging music and reminded me that I had only lasted three hours in a tent in Granny Clegg's garden: Hester's cats were pawing the canvas, it was terrifying.) Mark Lambert and the Kylies are going as well. I am staggered that they have been allowed to take GCSE French. Mark Lambert falls about laughing every time Ms Hopwood-White says 'Oui'. Hugo Thorndyke is right, school standards are falling.

. . . .

Wednesday 8

Mum is not happy about the Paris trip. She thinks it will be racked with teenage sex and alcohol. I think she has been panicked by Cherie and her 'urges' speech.

I pointed out that *a*) I had no intention of having sex with any of the morons in my year until I was at least sixteen, if ever and that *b*) it could harm my GCSE result if I didn't go. Mum said she would think about it. Anyway—there is no chance of me being a teenage mother until I get my period, which is still freakishly absent.

. . . .

Thursday 9
The shopkeepers of Saffron Walden have followed the lead of fellow shopping Meccas Lakeside and Bluewater and have banned hood-wearing. It is on the front page of the *Walden Chronicle*. Mum says it is a vital blow for anti-social youths.

. . . .

Friday 10
Mum is writing to the council and to the Saffron Walden Chamber of Commerce to complain about the hood ban. She was ousted from Boots for having the hood up on her cagoule. I took the opportunity of her being blinded by anger to get her to sign the Paris trip note. Now all I have to do is get a cheque off Dad.

. . . .

Saturday 11
Went round Sad Ed's to plan what we are going to do on our Paris trip. Ed is overexcited because some dead singer

143

is buried there. Ed said he isn't any old dead singer—he is Jim Morrison, legendary drug-abusing sexual deviant who died prematurely in mysterious circumstances. Ed is hoping some of these qualities are going to transfer through the grave into him. I said I didn't think Ms Hopwood-White would agree to visiting a graveyard but he said that Chopin was buried there as well so we could use that as a lure.

More importantly—what am I going to wear? I am not sure that the French appreciate vintage, let alone Brownie T-shirts. They all wear tight black things. I am going to have to persuade Scarlet to lend me her goth outfits.

Sunday 12

Went round Scarlet's. She is refusing to lend me goth clothes. She says she needs them for Glastonbury and that all she can spare is a pair of school plimsolls and a beret she wore on no-uniform day last year when she went as Che Guevara. She says it will be ironic.

Watched *The O.C.*, which was full of glamorous alcoholics and charity balls. I wish my mother was more American. She could stagger around the house in kitten heels and Gucci, clutching a champagne flute, instead of the Dettox spray which is usually welded into her hand.

Treena was round ours when I got back. Her bulimia is not working. She is definitely putting on weight.

Monday 13

Jewish Feast of Weeks

Something is wrong with Thin Kylie. She was suspiciously quiet at school and didn't even make a comment when Emily Reeve turned up wearing knee-length socks (not in a fashionable Japanese way). Now she is sitting on the front wall crying. Fat Kylie is trying to comfort her whilst simultaneously smoking a cigarette and eating a packet of Skittles.

Maybe I should try to befriend her. I could be like Cher in *Clueless* and mould her into a better person. Plus she might be a chav genius—like Ms Dynamite, only white. Yes—that is it! I am going to do a good deed and help her out of her meaningless existence. This is my one chance to make my life more Julie Burchill and less Enid Blyton.

5 p.m.

That did not go according to plan. Something very bad has happened. It turns out that the giant Justin Timberlake badge was significant and that Kylie's relationship with Mark Lambert has moved beyond the minky-touching stage but not, apparently, to the buying condoms stage because she needs the morning-after pill. I told her she could get it from the chemist but she said she had got it four times this month already and is on a blacklist at Boots and Superdrug. I said, couldn't Fat Kylie get it for her? (I didn't say 'Fat'.) But Fat Kylie said, 'I'm

Catholic, innit, I don't believe in contraception.' Then they both stared at me waiting for me to say something. Their tightly gelled hair and giant hooped earrings were so menacing I ended up offering to get the pill for Kylie. I have made a doctor's appointment for tomorrow lunchtime. Boots will never believe I am sixteen.

Tuesday 14

7 a.m.

Woke up feeling sick. I have made a terrible mistake trying to befriend someone from a council estate. Scarlet would never make me do this. But then Scarlet would never sleep with anyone without several methods of contraception, especially with Mark Lambert. Plus her dad is an abortionist so she has options. I thought about trying to get off school but, even if I did get past Mum's forensic vomit checks, the Kylies would kill me.

4 p.m.

I have done something truly awful. I have given Thin Kylie breath mints instead of the morning-after pill. It is Dr Potter's fault. She was away so I had to see Dr Braithwaite (huge hands; lazy eye; bottle of whisky in desk drawer) who plays golf with Dad and is renowned for his inability to abide by patient confidentiality rules. If I had asked for the morning-after pill half of Saffron

Walden would have known by tomorrow morning. So I feigned a stomach bug and got a prescription for milk of magnesia, and a lollipop (for not crying). But on my way back to school I had a vision of my life when Kylie found out so I diverted via home and told Mum I had a headache and that Mrs Leech had run out of painkillers following last week's inter-year hockey tournament. (It is surprisingly easy to lie when your life is under threat.) I had planned to give Kylie some vitamin tablets or something else harmless but possibly resembling morning after pills but all Mum had was bright pink liquid Calpol so I dispensed a load of Grandpa's Smint-type things into one of Mum's miniature Tupperware containers and took those back to school instead.

The Kylies were waiting in their headquarters (aka the lower school toilets). When I gave them the pot Thin Kylie said, 'They didn't look like that last time?' And Fat Kylie said, 'Why are there so many?' Why, oh why, didn't I check how many pills is normal? Any other nearly fourteen year old would be familiar with this kind of thing. I told her I had got her some for next time and changed the bottle so her mum wouldn't find out. Luckily, the Kylies are easily fooled—Thin Kylie said, 'Wicked,' and took one of the mints immediately.

Oh, God, I am a bad person. What if she really is pregnant? It will be all my fault. Maybe I can blame faulty drugs.

147

6 p.m.
What if Cherie threatens to sue the pill company? They will test the pills and find out they are no more potent than TicTacs. I am doomed.

Wednesday 15
Kylie was off school today. I hope she has not had a bad reaction to the mints.

Thursday 16
False alarm. She was in London at her mum's *X-Factor* audition. Cherie has no hope if her karaoke is anything to go by.

Friday 17
Am still in morning-after pill panic. Sad Ed and Scarlet asked me what was wrong. I lied and said the dog had got a miniature orc model stuck in its throat and might have to have an operation. I felt awful afterwards but if I tell them the truth they will be all weird anyway. Anyway, it is not a total lie, the dog did eat an orc but threw it up during *Countdown*.

Thin Kylie beat up Dean Denley, the one-eyed midget in Year Seven, at last break. I am hoping it is a sign of PMT.

Saturday 18

Tried to spy on Kylie from my bedroom but their Austrian blinds were in the way. James offered me his binoculars but I declined. I do not think even they can get past two metres of pink ruffle.

Sunday 19

Father's Day

Forgot Father's Day in the pill panic. Had to make an emergency outing to Mr Patel's (the only shop open at 7.45 a.m.) to buy a card. He had obviously experienced a last-minute rush as the choice was limited to a racing car design with 'from your loving son' inside or a giant padded Care Bear one with 'You're my best friend'. I chose the racing car one (£1.79). The padded one was £5.99. I will swap it with James.

10 a.m.

James had made Dad a card with a glued-on picture of Carol Vorderman (Dad's favourite intellectual TV presenter). He agreed to swap for £3.50 and my copy of *The Princess Diaries*. So it would have been cheaper and less weird to get the hideous padded bear card. Dad said the Carol Vorderman card was very artistic. He is good at lying. They teach him to do it at work.

Monday 20

It is SATS week. Oh, God. How could I have forgotten this as well? It is all the stress from Thin Kylie and her morning-after menaces. Mr Wilmott gave us a talk in Assembly how it wasn't about not letting the school down, it was about not letting ourselves down. That is rubbish. He is just worried about being replaced by a superhead like at Harold Wilson Modern in Bishop's Stortford (now the Burger King Sports Academy). I have English and Science tomorrow. I am going to have to revise all night.

7 p.m.

Have stocked up with banned Red Bull from Mr Patel (smuggled it into the house inside a pomegranate juice carton). Will start revising after *Watchdog*.

8 p.m.

James and dog have drunk all the pomegranate juice/Red Bull. They are disturbing my science revision by jumping on the bed next door and singing 'Light My Fire' (Will Young version).

8.15 p.m.

Not the dog, obviously. It is barking.

8.30 p.m.

Will just watch *You Are What You Eat*.

9 p.m.
And *Supernanny*.

10 p.m.
OK, am definitely going to revise. Have drunk two cups of Nescafé.

Tuesday 21

First day of summer
7 a.m.
Aaaagh. Nescafé was decaffeinated. It is all over. I am going to fail my SATS and get sent to a pupil referral unit. Actually that might be interesting. I bet they are full of misunderstood youths. Although I know Stacey O'Grady has been in one three times and he is not misunderstood, he really is an idiot.

James and the dog are still asleep. They did not go to bed until midnight. Mum thinks they might have diabetes. Or sleeping sickness. Have hidden the incriminating carton in the dustbin in case Mum finds it and dusts it for clues.

Will read *To Kill A Mockingbird* on the way to school to make up for lost time.

4 p.m.
Walked into lamppost trying to read on way to school and missed English exam due to blood pouring from gash on forehead. Then could not concentrate in science due to

151

itchy bandage haphazardly put on by Mrs Leech. So now am disfigured and a moron with the SAT results to prove it. Plus Thin Kylie is still showing no signs of having period and I know Fat Kylie is on because she had to leave the exam twice due to period pain. Although Sad Ed says it may be because she ate five packets of Skips in registration.

Wednesday 22

7 a.m.
Maths. At least you can't revise for maths. You either know it or you don't. That's what Sad Ed says anyway.

4 p.m.
Sad Ed is wrong. You can revise for maths. At least I would have known what a quadratic equation was if I had bothered to check last night. I am doomed. I will be at the bottom of the league table, condemning Mr Wilmott and John Major High with me.

Thursday 23

Scarlet has gone to Glastonbury. Suzy faked her a sick note claiming she had diarrhoea. Scarlet tried to get her to change it to TB but Suzy was adamant that diarrhoea was more convincing. Tony Blair has no hope of tackling truancy if would-be Labour MPs are going to flout the laws to take their children to drug-addled music festivals.

Thank God it is Paris tomorrow. Maybe the change of climate will bring on Thin Kylie's period. And even mine!

- -

Friday 24
10 p.m.

Am in Paris. Romance of city blighted only by having to share a room with Emily Reeve who has brought her entire doll collection with her. Sad Ed has a room of his own. This is because Mark Lambert said he might accidentally try to stab or maim Ed in his sleep as he is learning combat training with the ATC. Ms Hopwood-White, vaguely aided by hopeless student teacher Mr Vaughan (twenty-three; earring; Gitanes and possible drug habit) has put them at opposite ends of the Travotel corridor.

Tomorrow we are going to the Louvre and then the Eiffel Tower. I expect they will be full of long-haired mysterious French students who want to whisk vintage English girls off to drink espressos by the Seine. It is a shame my hotel window does not have a view of Paris by night, as advertised on the hotel's website. Instead it has a view of the hotel bin area, which is not at all picturesque.

- -

Saturday 25

Midnight

Oh, my God! Fat Kylie is having an illicit affair with Mark Lambert. It is like Brad and Jennifer and Angelina but with ugly fourteen year olds. Here is how the drama unfolds:

8 a.m.

Kylies' sleeping arrangements amended after they drank the entire minibar at a cost of €78.48 (my calculations— they should give you questions like that in the SATS, it is far more useful than quadratic equations). I am now sharing with Thin Kylie, and Fat Kylie is in with Emily Reeve. This is not ideal but at least I can keep a close eye on her menstrual cycle.

9 a.m.

Absence of Mr Vaughan noted.

9.15 a.m.

Mr Vaughan roused from Gitanes and Pernod stupor by Sad Ed.

9.30 a.m.

Class takes le Metro under guidance of Ms Hopwood-White and Mr Vaughan.

9.40 a.m.

Class exits le Metro so Mr Vaughan can be sick on le platform.

10 a.m.
Mr Vaughan is revived by pain au chocolat, purchased by Sad Ed, and miniature whisky, stolen by Mark Lambert, and class boards le Metro again.

10 a.m.–10.50 a.m.
Class circles Paris on le Metro looking for correct stop.

11 a.m.
Class arrives at Louvre.

11.30 a.m.
Class asked to leave Louvre due to overexcitement at nude paintings.

12 noon
Thin Kylie refuses to eat in authentic brasserie 'Les Deux Puces' because she is 'allergic to garlic and frogs'.

1 p.m.
Class eats in McDonald's on Champs Élysée.

1.15 p.m.
Class leaves McDonald's following pommes frites fight with boys' school from Edinburgh. Ms Hopwood-White seen commiserating in toilet corridor with sexy Scottish boys' school teacher.

2 p.m.
Class arrives at Eiffel Tower queue.

3.30 p.m.
Class leaves Eiffel Tower queue in disgust and goes souvenir shopping at famous French department store Galeries Lafayette.

4.30 p.m.
Class asked to leave Galeries Lafayette after incident involving Thin Kylie and Mark Lambert and the lingerie changing rooms.

6 p.m.
Class eats authentic French chips and pizza from Travotel revolving buffet.

7 p.m.
Ms Hopwood-White seen leaving Travotel in company of sexy Scottish teacher.

7.05 p.m.
Sad Ed leaves Travotel via bin area on Jim Morrison pilgrimage.

7.15 p.m.
Rest of class watch screening of *Maid in Manhattan* (dubbed in French, no subtitles) in

Conference Room A (aka canteen) under supervision of Mr Vaughan.

8.00 p.m.
Screening of *Maid in Manhattan* abandoned due to riot following heated debate on size of Jennifer Lopez's bottom and class sent to rooms for night by hotel manager after Mr Vaughan found asleep on back row.

9.30 p.m.
Thin Kylie complains of stomach ache and possible French Big Mac/Travotel revolving buffet poisoning.

9.35 p.m.
Thin Kylie sick in bidet.

9.40 p.m.
Room service called to clean up vomit.

11 p.m.
Room service arrive to clean up vomit.

11.15 p.m.
Ms Hopwood-White seen entering hotel with sexy Scottish teacher via bin area.

11.30 p.m.
Sexy Scottish teacher seen leaving Travotel via bin area.

11.40 p.m.
Thin Kylie demands presence of Fat Kylie and sends Rachel Riley to find her.

11.41 p.m.
Emily Reeve (in My Little Pony nightdress) tells Rachel Riley that Fat Kylie has not been seen since dispersal of *Maid in Manhattan* screening.

11.45 p.m.
Fat Kylie traced via distinctive grunting sounds to Mark Lambert's room at far end of Travotel corridor.

11.50 p.m.
Rachel Riley informs Thin Kylie that Fat Kylie is in bed and cannot be disturbed. (Not a total lie.)

11.55 p.m.
Ms Hopwood-White bangs on doors to tell everyone to *'fermez les bouches'*.

Sunday 26
8 a.m.
I am racked with indecision. Should I tell Thin Kylie about the illicit sex and get beaten up by Fat Kylie and

possibly stabbed by Mark Lambert or keep quiet and
end up getting morning-after pills for Fat Kylie as
well? It is like *Sophie's Choice*. Or Hobson's. Who was
Hobson?

Plus Sad Ed is still missing. Ms Hopwood-White has
gone to find him. I told Mr Vaughan he had gone on a
pilgrimage to see Jim Morrison's grave but he said
everyone knows Jim Morrison isn't really buried there—
and that he probably isn't even dead but is fat and living
in Las Vegas with Elvis. I said that was a bit far-fetched
but he said, 'No one saw the body—how do you explain
that?' (Mr Vaughan is conspiracy theory mad—he thinks
Diana was killed by Prince Philip for wearing cleavage-
revealing dresses.) We are under strict instructions not to
leave the Travotel. Ms Hopwood-White is terrified she
might lose more students and end up in the *Daily Mail*.

11 a.m.
Sad Ed is back. He had been arrested for defacing Jim
Morrison's grave with chewing gum and a Mars bar
wrapper. He claims it was a poem but the policeman
couldn't read English and then a pigeon pecked it to get at
the chocolate and it blew away so the evidence was gone.

Why, oh why, didn't I go with him? I could have spent
the night in a foreign jail with nothing to eat and the
howls of tortured inmates ringing in my ears instead of the
sound of Fat Kylie and Mark Lambert having sex. Ed said
that actually they gave him a falafel and four pain au

chocolates and he got to read a French porn mag. That is what is wrong with the French. They are too lax with their criminals. Inspector Morse would never have let his suspects read porn. We are all going home on an early train. Ms Hopwood-White says it is worth the supplement.

I feel sorry for Thin Kylie. Not only is she possibly pregnant due to my evil Smint/morning-after pill changeover but now the father of the illegitimate child is secretly having relations with her clinically obese alleged best friend. Trisha would have a field day. She could devote a whole show to it. She could call it 'Leave the underage father of my baby alone, fat friend!'

10 p.m.
Back home. Mum asked if my trip had been educational. I said it had. Luckily Ms Hopwood-White has promised not to tell anyone about Sad Ed getting arrested. This is insurance against Sad Ed telling Mr Wilmott that she broke school trip regulations by sneaking out of hotel to meet up with sexy Scottish teacher and leaving inept Mr Vaughan in charge.

Monday 27
Went round Scarlet's at lunchtime. She was off school due to pneumonia and a mild dose of trench foot following unseasonal downpours at Glastonbury. She was in bed with henna tattoos and hair braids listening to

goth music. She looked like a sickly ethnic vampire. She said Glastonbury was life-changing and that she is in love with a juggler called Axe. I asked her if they had done it and she said no, but he had let her hold his fire clubs. He lives in a bivouac in a forest near Brighton. This is typical. And totally unfair.

Tuesday 28
Thank God. Thin Kylie is not pregnant. She asked if she could 'lend' a Tampax during science. I said 'borrow' and she said, 'Well, I ain't giving it back, you perv, am I.' Then I said I didn't have any (obviously) so she had to get a giant sanitary towel off Mrs Leech. I cannot go through this worry every month. I am going to have to get the pills back.

Wednesday 29
The school is overrun with Andy Murray madness. I do not understand it—he is tall and geeky. Just because he has an iPod does not make him a sex symbol. Although he is marginally better than Tim Henman whose head is oversized. Even James is demanding tennis lessons (Mum has said no on the grounds that he has shown no promise at Swingball.) I predict this craze will be over by July and the tennis courts of Saffron Walden will be overgrown and used for football practice once again.

Told Kylie I needed the morning-after pills. She said they were round Fat Kylie's so we would have to go to Whiteshot Estate tomorrow (Fat Kylie is off school with alleged mumps). I agreed. It is the only way to end this Smint contraception mess. Have told Mum I am going to a rounders team try-out. She looked suspicious. She knows I have the upper body strength of a kitten.

* *

Thursday 30

Went round Fat Kylie's to get Smints. The house was full of children. They were all drinking Um Bongo and watching MTV on their giant plasma screen, except Whitney, who was busy sharing a Peperami with Tupac. Mrs O'Grady was not present. Whitney, who is named after Kylie's dead dad's favourite singer, is suspiciously brown. I noted that, in addition to the plasma TV, the O'Gradys also owned three PlayStations, an extensive DVD library of Steven Seagal films, a Barbie scooter and a Nissan 4x4 with a 'Honk if you're horny' sticker on the rear window (I have seen Mrs O'Grady and I do not think she gets many honks). Granny Clegg is right, the benefits system is too generous.

Fat Kylie got the pills while Thin Kylie and I watched *Bump and Grind* with the feral children. One of them, possibly Brady, tried to hug me, leaving Dairylea Dunkables smeared on my uniform. Thin Kylie told me to be careful as he is renowned for weeing on people. Then

Fat Kylie came back and I ate the remaining seventeen Smints immediately. Thin Kylie said, 'Jesus, Riley, who did you shag, the entire maths club?' (She has no understanding of medicine, or my taste in boys.) I said, 'Something like that.' So now my reputation exceeds even Leanne Jones who actually did shag three of the senior maths club last year. She got an A* in her maths GCSE. It was the only exam she passed.

When I got home Mum saw the Dairylea Dunkables stain and accused me of illicit eating of junk food. She made me take the skirt off in the kitchen, in front of James and Mumtaz (who were eating health-giving yoghurt) so she could prevent permanent staining. I figured the truth was worse so I just apologized and said I was going to read in my room. I note she did not ask me how my alleged rounders trial went, which shows how low her expectations are of my sporting prowess.

Friday 1

Thin Kylie has found out about Fat Kylie and Mark Lambert. Fat Kylie made the fatal mistake of coming to school with the evidence of Mark Lambert's sexual attentions on her outsize Primark jacket (an 'I ♥ 50 Cent' badge). They arranged to fight it out on the sheep field at lunchtime. So the whole school trooped up there, but by the time the Kylies had taken off all their giant hoops and rings (illegal fighting implements under unwritten John Major High rules) Mrs Brain had reported suspiciously low chip and doughnut sales and Mr Wilmott arrived to break it up. Mark Lambert is pleading partial innocence. He says he couldn't help it, he had needs and Thin Kylie was being sick in a bidet from le Big Mac poisoning. Ms Hopwood-White is on Thin Kylie's side. She said men are all liars and cheats and should be castrated. I think she has broken up with the sexy Scottish teacher. The long distance must have torn them apart. Scarlet says that is why Axe has not rung her. I pointed out that it was only 104 miles to Brighton via the M25 (James checked on Dad's AA route planner) but she said it is a thousand when you are in love, plus there are roadworks on the A24.

Saturday 2

Scarlet is going to Live 8. Suzy is overexcited as she and Bob went to the one twenty years ago. She still wears the

T-shirt despite it having revealing cigarette burns on the nipple area. Sad Ed and I are going to watch it on telly instead (Mum and Dad are going to the garden centre, Grandpa and Treena are babysitting). Sad Ed says it is a moment of musical history. Personally I think his expectations may be a bit too high. Mariah Carey is playing.

5 p.m.
Live 8 viewing has ended. Mum got back and found Grandpa drinking cider and blackcurrant, the dog eating her mung bean cultivator, and James and Treena dancing provocatively to Mariah Carey. She said it was a scene from her worst nightmare. She has weird dreams.

. . . .

Sunday 3

Thin Kylie came over today to 'hang out'. I don't think she has any friends any more. Fat Kylie claimed Tracey Hughes and Lynn Herbert for her gang following the falling-out, which left Thin Kylie with Lynn Start, but she has defected to her sister's gang in Year Ten. She is their mascot. Mum did not look pleased when she opened the door. She does not approve of the Britchers. She says they are lowering the tone of the neighbourhood with their incessant arguing and the St George flag that Terry has put up in one of the bedroom windows.

Kylie said my room needed a makeover. She said all the pictures of ugly and dead women (Sylvia Plath and

Ophelia) gave her the creeps and was a 'bit lesbo'. She says I should stand up for my rights to have telly in my room as well and suggested I threaten to bunk off or not do homework. She says it has got her a new stereo and a trip to Alton Towers in the last month. Which is amazing as she is always bunking off and not doing homework anyway, so Mrs Britcher is being blackmailed under totally false pretences.

Then she got bored with the lack of TV so we went down to Barry Island to watch Darryl Stamp and his mates rev up their crap cars. (He has finished his community sentence for robbing Mr Patel's. He had to look after some goats at Harlow Town Farm. No wonder re-offending is so high. Pet Corner is hardly going to turn someone off a life of crime.) Darryl offered me and Kylie a joyride to Bishop's Stortford in his Fiesta but I said I had to get back for Sunday lunch. Kylie went anyway. She is mad. The car has no wing mirrors and a purple neon light underneath it so it looks like a really crap spaceship. There would be nothing joyful about riding in it. When I got back, Mum said she hoped I wasn't going to make a habit of 'playing' with Kylie. I pointed out that she should be pleased because at least Kylie's mum wasn't a vegetarian sex therapist. But she said she'd rather that than someone who thinks Kraft Cheese Slices are a cocktail canapé.

And I forgot to go round Scarlet's, as prearranged during exceptionally dull citizenship lesson. Scarlet rang

169

up to demand to know why. I told her the dog had eaten my watch. I have to stop telling lies. It is getting confusing.

. . . .

Monday 4

Kylie ate her Turkey Twizzlers with me at lunchtime. I had no choice in the matter. She sat down before Sad Ed could get to the chair (his weight is a speed impediment). He went to join Scarlet on the hummus table instead, even though he had chicken surprise (the surprise is the lack of chicken). Luckily Mrs Brain did not notice or there could have been another free-meals-table-style stand-off. (Discussion of which pencilled in for PTA on Thursday night, according to Mum. She is for segregation.) I am being torn between my friends. It is like *West Side Story*.

. . . .

Tuesday 5

Not a good day. Rumours are rife about me and the maths club. Thin Kylie says Fat Kylie started them as revenge. Ali Hassan is refusing to speak to me in case it incriminates him further. He is worried his parents will be thrown out of the Church of England. I don't think he has anything to worry about. Reverend Begley will take anyone. I have even seen him trying to convert Barry the Blade. Scarlet is livid that I did not tell her. I said it was all a mistake involving some Smints and the Kylies but she says there is no smoke without fire. Sad Ed just looked sad.

Wednesday 6

Andy Murray madness has officially ended. London has won the Olympics for 2012. James now wants to train as a speed cyclist. I pointed out he will still be only fifteen when it is the Olympics but he said he would campaign to get the age lowered for that as well as Parliament.

Suzy rang to offer me sexual advice. I told her I was the victim of a vicious hate campaign started by an obese adulteress. Plus, just because I was nearly fourteen did not mean I was doing 'it' and that, unlike several of my peers, I intended to abide by the age of consent. She seemed disappointed.

Thursday 7

London has been blown up by suicide bombers. Mum says it goes to show she was right to stay in Saffron Walden, which has been, historically, major-incident free, unless you count the St George's Day fracas. Grandpa Clegg rang to shout about swivel-eyed malcontents (he means Muslims). He says he is thinking of turning the outside loo into an air-raid shelter. I think he wound Mum into a foreigner-fearing frenzy because she told James that Mumtaz couldn't come over for tea tomorrow.

Plus, the PTA meeting got cancelled due to the potential terror threat so the free school meals debacle is destined to remain unresolved until September. Personally I think Mr Wilmott is over-reacting. I do not think Al Qaeda will be targeting John Major High anytime soon.

Friday 8

Tonight's 'end of year' school disco has been postponed as a mark of respect for the London bombings. It has been rescheduled for next Friday when Mr Wilmott thinks the 'hoo-ha' will have calmed down a bit.

Saturday 9

Thin Kylie has given me a makeover. She has dyed my hair using her mum's Sun In spray and straightened it. She says I look like Brittany Murphy instead of the 'ugly one out of *Scooby Doo*' now. Maybe that is what was wrong. Maybe tragic heroines just need a decent hairdo and some lipgloss. I do feel better. Although that may change when Mum and James get back from Waitrose.

5 p.m.

Mum has added hair dye to her banned list. I tried to explain the Brittany Murphy thing but she said the only person I looked like was Vanessa Feltz and then she made me go and use her Head and Shoulders to try and lessen the dye. It did not work. Now I look like Barbara Windsor. Although I am at least dandruff free. Even James is on her side. He says hair dye is the first sign of juvenile delinquency and that I will be heading for an ASBO if I am not careful. Scarlet and Sad Ed will understand. They wear eyeliner.

Sunday 10

Went round Scarlet's for the second annual *O.C.* final episode ceremony. Jack answered the door. He said, 'Why, Miss Riley. You really are beautiful,' and then burst out laughing. Scarlet was horrified. She said blonde hair is anathema to goths. Sad Ed was not happy either. He says I am mixing in bad company and will be listening to R and B next. Everyone is turning into my mum. They do not understand. They will be jealous when Thin Kylie turns out to be a working-class literary marvel. Though I must say I am anxious for her to start showing signs of this. At the moment her reading is limited to gossip magazines.

Monday 11

My new hair is the centre of much hilarity at school. So far I have been likened to: Vera Duckworth, Lily Savage, and Fat Kylie's poodle Tupac. I bet Peaches Geldof doesn't have to put up with this kind of harassment. She is the style icon for our generation and is probably allowed to smoke and drink wine at dinner. Whereas I still own a Brownies T-shirt and am not allowed to drink Ribena except under strict supervision in outside spaces.

Tuesday 12
Battle of the Boyne
Holiday (N. Ire.)

It is Mum's birthday tomorrow. I have got her a new mung bean cultivator. I am going to sign it from me and the dog in the hope it will get us both back into her good books.

Wednesday 13
Mum's birthday

Mum got a mung bean cultivator (me and the dog), a Cif gift pack (James), an M&S voucher (Dad), a bottle of Britney Spears perfume (Grandpa and Treena), and £5 and a UKIP car sticker (Granny and Grandpa Clegg). Auntie Joyless did not send anything. She is still of the opinion our family is beyond redemption.

Thursday 14

Mum has a rash all over her neck and face. She looks like Nigel Moore in Year Eleven who has impetigo (not potato blight, as claimed by Mark Lambert). It is the Britney Spears perfume. Grandpa admitted Treena got it in the White Horse off someone called Ducatti Mick. Mum has listed him in her ASBO catalogue.

Friday 15

St Swithin's Day

It is the end of year school disco tonight. I am going to wear my vintage (Monsoon) skirt and Brownie T-shirt (worn inside-out, as seen on Peaches Geldof in *Bliss* magazine last month). With my newly blonde hair I will look just like Sienna Miller. Justin Statham is definitely going, according to Scarlet. Although she didn't seem as enthusiastic about telling me this as she normally would. Maybe she is still pining after Axe. I must be careful not to flaunt my prospective love life in front of her.

11 p.m.

Disco did not go according to plan. I did not look at all like Sienna Miller. Kylie came over after tea and persuaded me to cut a metre off the bottom of the Monsoon skirt and borrow her mum's halter top so the closest resemblance was Paris Hilton with a perm. She said, 'I ain't going out with someone with no second-hand shit on, someone might have, like, died in it. Gross.'

When we got to school, Scarlet said I couldn't stand with her in Goth Corner (aka next to the out-of-order fire extinguishers) or she and Sad Ed might get ejected. (Sad Ed was allowed to stand there because he had a black T-shirt on). So I had to stand with Thin Kylie and help her give Fat Kylie and Mark Lambert the evils. Luckily that did not last long as they got sent home for inappropriate behaviour behind the crash mats. Then Kylie danced (snogged, with his hands up her boob tube) with Jason Kinsey who is in Criminals and Retards for trying to set fire to Rat Corner. Having a reputation as a nymphomaniac certainly boosts your popularity for slow dances. I got offers from four members of the science club and Gary Fletcher off the Waitrose pet food aisle who is in Year Eleven and has done it with Leanne Jones. I declined all and stood with Sad Ed at the 'bar' (Ms Hopwood-White's Coke stall). Scarlet was dancing with head goth Trevor Pledger who has a floor-length leather coat—the holy grail of gothwear. Sad Ed said he preferred my old look. I said it wasn't my idea and he said, 'To thine own self be true.' Which is out of *Clueless*. He is still trying to be poetic in everyday situations. Then they played The Killers and I danced with Ed for a bit, which was weirdly nice. But then Scarlet came over and said she and Ed had to go back to Goth Corner as Daisy Devlin was going to show everyone her fake tattoo of Marilyn Manson on her left buttock. I got bored and went home. Thin Kylie was in the staff car park with one hand down Jason Kinsey's trousers. She said she would get a lift on his minibike.

When I got in Mum went mental at me for walking on my own. I pointed out that, given the fact that it was still broad daylight, and we lived in Saffron Walden, I was not likely to get mugged or raped. But ever since Granny Clegg told her the government is rehousing paedophiles in suburbia she is paranoid and made me promise to phone Dad for a lift next time. I told her I couldn't as I didn't have a mobile and Mr Wilmott has banned pupil use of the staffroom phone after Stacey O'Grady called a sexline. (He claimed it was a legitimate emergency.) Then I went upstairs before she could think of a clever answer.

At least it did not rain. Which is good news weather-wise for the next forty days.

Saturday 16

Treena came over. She was wearing jogging bottoms again. She is too fat to fit into her jeans. If she lets herself go any further Grandpa will ditch her. I have caught him eyeing Cherie over the road. So has Mum. She has threatened to move his bedroom to the dining room where he will only overlook Marjory's ornamental water feature.

Scarlet and Sad Ed went to the fair on the common without inviting me. James told me he saw them on the ghost train with some other goths. (Dad took him and Mumtaz and the dog. The dog ate three lots of candyfloss and a toffee apple and was sick on a giant saucer after it leapt onto the Mad Hatter's Tea Party under-tens merry-go-round in pursuit of James. Dad has vowed never to go again.)

Sunday 17

Kylie came over with *Cosmopolitan* so we went to my bedroom and did the sex survey. I got mostly *d*'s ('Nun') and she got mostly *a*'s ('Madonna'). She knows a terrifying amount about penises.

Then Sad Ed knocked on the window. He had climbed up Dad's ladder, left out after trying to readjust the aerial so Grandpa could watch *Home and Away* on Channel 5. Kylie opened the window and said, 'What do you think this is, *Dawson's* f**king *Creek*, you fat weirdo?' He said he had tried the door but the doorbell battery had gone and he couldn't rouse Grandpa from his post-Sunday lunch torpor in front of the Grand Prix (Mum and Dad had taken James to B&Q to buy a shelf for his expanding doll collection).

Kylie demanded to know what he was doing so he handed me a CD and said it was a pre-birthday present. Kylie told him he had better go as the ladder 'wasn't licensed for bloaters'.

Then Sad Ed said, 'To thine own self be true' again so Kylie called him a poof and slammed the window shut, narrowly missing his fingers. I wish he would stop spouting *Clueless* all the time. It doesn't help his image.

Then Kylie looked at the CD and said, 'Oh my God, it was Fat Ed what got you nearly pregnant!' I said it was 'who, not what', and that anyway it wasn't him, and told her to give me the CD back, but she waved it around chanting, 'You shagged Fat Ed, admit it, admit it!' repeatedly.

So then, and I only did this to shut her up, I told her he was gay and snogging Jonah Reed (who once played Mary in a primary school nativity and is therefore destined to be classified as gay for ever). Kylie was so shocked she dropped the CD down the back of the bed. I begged her not to tell anyone as Sad Ed hadn't 'come out' yet and his parents were Aled Jones fans and might take it badly. She promised her lips were sealed, but she said that after Lynn Start told her she had a third nipple and the whole school was calling her 'triple tits' by first break the next day. I may have made a fatal mistake. Sad Ed is going to kill me.

Monday 18

Mark Lambert has run away with the fair that was on the common at the weekend. It is all over the school. He is going to spin waltzers, according to Fat Kylie. She is devastated. He tried to get her to go with him but she said she didn't want to 'live in a caravan with some gyppos'. This is rich. She goes to a caravan park in Clacton every summer with her horde of feral siblings. Thin Kylie is comforting her. They are reunited in their grief.

More worryingly, Jude Law has cheated on Sienna with a commoner—his nanny. If even the glorious and vintage Sienna is not immune to lying and cheating then what hope is there for us mere mortals? Not that I am going out with anyone for them to be able to cheat on me.

Tuesday 19

The Sad Ed gay rumours have started. Fat Kylie stuck a picture of Graham Norton on his locker and Oona Rickets has invited him to join her Gay and Lesbian and Proud Association. Ed told her he was neither. Thank God Mark Lambert is not here to add his voice to the bigoted throng. Sad Ed says he doesn't care because all poetic geniuses are persecuted during their short but tragic lives. I am not sure how long this devil-may-care attitude will last in the face of the right-wing leanings of John Major High school governors, not to mention his parents. Then he asked if I had listened to the CD yet. I had to admit that I hadn't. It is still behind the bed due to the panic following the gay revelations.

9 p.m.

Found CD under bed. Unfortunately so had the dog and it is now chewed beyond recognition. It was probably only full of songs about death anyway. I have given it to James to use for his light-refracting CD mobile (as featured on *Blue Peter*).

Wednesday 20

Sad Ed has been forced to issue a vigorous denial of any homosexual leanings after Jonah Reed's mum wrote a letter to Ms Hopwood-White demanding that he use the girls' changing rooms for PE. He says he is not taking his clothes off in front of sixty-seven girls as they will be too critical of his physique. He is right. It is a good thing it is the last day of school on Friday. So far the source of the rumours has not been identified but I fear Thin Kylie may blab to Fat Kylie then it will all be over.

Thursday 21

Thin Kylie blabbed. Scarlet stormed up to me in first break and demanded to know if I was claiming one of my best friends was gay to boost my popularity in the chav hierarchy. I said on the contrary, the chavs are no friends of gays and lesbians and anyway, Sad Ed might be gay, we just might not know it yet. She said he was far from gay and was in love with some stupid cow who was too obsessed with herself and her image to notice. (She must mean Sophie Jacobs. That would explain why he hates Justin Statham so much.) Then she said I had totally changed and she didn't think she could be my friend any more and stormed off with her Glastonbury goth skirt tinkling its bells angrily.

I will give her a while to calm down then I will go and explain everything. She will understand that I was lured into it by Thin Kylie.

It would be good if Sad Ed was gay though. We could be like *Will and Grace*. Maybe the Sophie Jacobs thing is a cover up. He does watch *The O.C.* and is good at clothes advice. Oh my God, it has been staring me in the face all along. Sad Ed is the key to Jacqueline Wilson-ing my life.

I am going to spend more time with him. That is if he is still speaking to me. Maybe he will thank me instead. I will prove instrumental in him coming out to his parents. They will embrace his alternative lifestyle and join Oona Rickets's club with him and get Aled Jones to be patron.

Friday 22

Sad Ed is not thanking me so far. He and Scarlet are not speaking to me. Though I did catch Sad Ed looking at me in maths so maybe he is cracking. But then Scarlet saw him and hit him with her set square.

I was glad to get out of school. The corridors were plagued by gangs of Year Elevens with cans of silly string and huddles of sixth form girls weeping because they are never going to see each other again (not until resits, anyway). Am going to have to win back Scarlet and Sad Ed soon or I am doomed to spend my summer holiday sitting on a wall with the Kylies drinking alcopops.

Plus James has commandeered the stereo and keeps playing a vintage love song compilation CD. It is unbearable. Since when did he like David Bowie? Plus it keeps getting stuck. The dog must have bitten it.

Saturday 23

Went round Scarlet's to make up but Jack answered the door and said she wasn't speaking to me. I begged him to let me in but he said Scarlet had threatened to put incriminating Celine Dion tracks on his iPod if he did. I said I would try Sad Ed instead. Jack said I shouldn't bother as he was upstairs with Scarlet as Scarlet couldn't trust him if he was on his own. I said it was like *Mean Girls* with me as Lindsay Lohan and Jack agreed.

3 p.m.
Ooh—maybe Jack thinks I look like Lindsay Lohan.

4 p.m.
Read *Cosmopolitan*, left by Thin Kylie. Am going to wax my bikini line. Apparently using Dad's Bic on my legs and armpits is not enough in these summer months.

Sunday 24
Bought wax from Waitrose. Thank God they open on a Sunday or I may well have been forced to have an untamed pubic area for another shameful day. Am going to do waxing after lunch.

3 p.m.
Am in agony. Cannot sit down properly due to bleeding of hair follicles in close proximity to minky. I followed the instructions properly but their warnings 'mild discomfort' are clearly inadequate. I may well write to complain. Told

Mum I had to lie down due to stomach ache. I do not want hair removal added to her banned list or I will look like Oona Rickets within a week. Will wear shorts in future or a sarong.

Monday 25

Went round Sad Ed's at 9 a.m. in a bid to thwart Scarlet (she does not get up until *T4* has finished). But his mum said he had stayed the night at a friend's (i.e. Scarlet's). Her vengeance knows no bounds. She is trying to steal my possibly gay best friend for herself so she can be Debra Messing and I will be the midget one with the high voice. It is not fair. Something must be done.

Took the dog for a walk past Scarlet's in the hope of catching her as she came out of the front door and having a reunion on the block-paved driveway. But after the seventh walk past Jack came out and told me I was wasting my time as they were punting in Cambridge with Bob and Suzy. He invited me in for tea but I said the dog might get overexcited by their two cats (Tony and Gordon) so I had better go home.

When I got back the Kylies were on the front wall listening to gangster rap so I joined them until Mum got back from Boots and gave me a look so menacing it actually made Thin Kylie shiver.

Tuesday 26

Have resigned myself to spending the summer holidays

184

with the Kylies. It will give Scarlet and Ed time to realize that their lives are meaningless without me in them. It could be good anyway. Cherie is getting a swimming pool installed in their back garden tomorrow. She says it is a symbol of their new position in life. Mum says it is a symbol of having more money than sense. They cost a fortune to run and you only use them for a few weeks a year. This is the same argument she used against me getting a pony and Dad getting a convertible MG.

Wednesday 27

The swimming pool is in. It is like a giant kidney-shaped washing-up bowl (why does everyone want to swim in something shaped like an organ that makes wee?) and is wide enough to do three breaststrokes across it. Kylie didn't actually get in the water. She says the chlorine could damage her hair. She and Cherie lay on the patio and read *Hello* instead. It is a good job I did wax my bikini line. The costume Cherie lent me is perilously high cut. (She said my navy and yellow Speedo would make Caprice look like Marjory and was best off in the bin.)

7 p.m.

Kylie was right about the chlorine. My hair now has a weird green tinge to it.

Thursday 28

Swam some more. Fat Kylie was there with Whitney. Cherie floated her round the pool on a pair of inflatable breasts. (Whitney, not Fat Kylie. She would have sunk them.) I expect it is the closest Whitney has got to that part of the anatomy. I have only ever seen her drink Yazoo and Coke. Read *Hot Stars*, *Grazia*, and *Heat*. Tried to initiate a discussion on Sienna Miller's new haircut but the Kylies were too busy assessing Jade Goody's boob job. I miss Scarlet and Sad Ed.

Friday 29

Swam. Ate Kraft cheese slices. Read *Heat*. It is amazing how doing nothing can stretch to a whole day.

Saturday 30

Oh my God. I am a real-life criminal. It is all Thin Kylie's fault. She made me do it. We ran out of Diet Coke (me) and Benson and Hedges (her and Cherie) at the pool so we went to Mr Patel's to get some but she didn't have enough money (I expect it is all in an offshore account. Rich people never have small change, it is a well known fact) so when Mr Patel bent down to get a bag for the Coke she grabbed a packet of cigarettes and put them in my pocket (she was wearing a tube dress and, to be fair, it would have been too obvious, whereas I had a capacious gypsy skirt on). But

186

Mr Patel must have eyes in the back of his head and demanded to search us. Kylie said no perv was going to touch her up so Mr Patel said he was going to call the police at which point I panicked and gave the cigarettes up.

Kylie feigned innocence by saying, 'Oh my God, my friend's a f**king burglar.' I pointed out that this was petty theft as opposed to burglary but I don't think that helped my case. I offered to make it up to Mr Patel by doing a Sunday paper round for free but he said he only has seven and he does them in his people carrier as most people get theirs from the petrol station at Tesco. He made me tell him my home phone number and called it there and then. James answered. He said, 'Send her home, she will be punished.'

When I got home, Mum lost the plot completely. She has sent me to my room to reflect on my delinquency while she and Dad think of a suitable punishment. James is right. My life is on a downward spiral. It will be drugs and tattoos next.

Sunday 31

Mum and Dad have decided to send me to Granny Clegg's for the rest of the summer to keep me away from the Kylies. They are going to stay in Saffron Walden. Dad is taking the day off work on Tuesday to drive me.

I do not want to go to Granny Clegg's. There is no internet, no Channel 5 reception, and no Channel 4 (the

TV can receive it but Granny Clegg thinks it is a force of corruption). Plus I will have to see Auntie Joyless and her freakish offspring.

It is my birthday tomorrow. I do not hold out much hope for any of requested presents (i.e. mobile phone).

Monday 1

Bank Holiday (Scotland)

My birthday

Presents received:

- Mum and Dad—a mobile phone! It is Pay As You Go and does not have a camera plus it is on the large side but it is a mobile phone none the less. Mum said it is so she and Dad can trace me at all times. I might have known the only way to break her was to turn it into an essential anti-ASBO item. Clearly crime does pay.

Also received:

- James—Carol Vorderman Sudoku Puzzle Book (several puzzles completed)
- Grandpa and Treena—a copy of *Bliss* magazine and a box of mint Matchmakers (both last-minute Mr Patel purchases, according to James)
- The dog—a copy of *How I Live Now* by Meg Rosoff. It is about a girl who is sent to live with her backward relatives in the middle of nowhere and then falls in love with her cousin. I hope the dog (aka Mum) is not encouraging me to seek solace in the arms of Boaz.
- Granny and Grandpa Clegg—Cornish phrases tea towel (am going to learn them later to help me acclimatize to the back of beyond)
- Sad Ed—nothing.
- Scarlet—nothing.

191

Thin Kylie came over to say happy birthday but James sent her away. She left me a novelty rude card and a bottle of Bacardi Breezer (both now confiscated).

Texted Scarlet with my new phone but got no reply. Thought maybe she was out of the country at an Ashram or something so texted Jack to test theory. He texted back saying she was in her bedroom doing Sad Ed's make-up and avoiding a suntan (the goth's worst nightmare). So she is still not speaking to me. Texted Jack to say I was being sent to Cornwall to reform. He said, 'BWARE RESTLESS NATIVES W SHARPENED PASTIES CU SOON X J.' Not sure whether the X is a kiss or a mistext. He does have long fingernails (essential guitar-playing accessory).

Exile begins tomorrow. Maybe it will not be so bad. Maybe village life will be wholesome and amusing like *Last of the Summer Wine*. Or possibly Rick Stein will have opened a bistro in St Slaughter and it will be flooded with cosmopolitan types.

Tuesday 2
First day of exile
8.45 p.m.
Am in Cornwall in Granny Clegg's spare bedroom (mauve bedspread, picture of blue-faced lady, overpowering smell of Fray Bentos). Have gone to bed already due to lack of *a*) decent television; *b*) stimulating

conversation; and *c*) mobile phone reception. Am going to climb up hill in village tomorrow to attempt contact with the outside world. No sign of Rick Stein bistro. Or of jovial *Last of the Summer Wine* types. Although there was a man actually chewing straw outside the Spar.

Journey was six hours of Radio 2 hell. I did not know my dad knows all the words to so many crap songs. Only the dog seemed sad to see me leave. Grandpa refused to let it come in case Granny Clegg seized it and held it hostage.

Wednesday 3
Exile—day two
10 a.m.
Went on cultural walk round sights of St Slaughter i.e. Spar and the Community Playground (disused). I do not see the point of Cornwall if it isn't by the sea. Plus there is no mobile phone reception in entire village. Pig-faced man with barely understandable accent said I would have to get closer to Redruth to pick anything up. I do not want to get closer to Redruth. It is like a giant Whiteshot Estate but with pasties. Besides, Granny and Grandpa Clegg do not have a car. They rely on Auntie Joyless's dented Metro.

1 p.m.
Ate lunch. Fishpaste sandwich and Viennetta.

3 p.m.
Raining.

5 p.m.
Still raining. Ate tea. Steak and kidney pie and tinned peaches. Asked Granny Clegg what she does all day to pass the time. She says she enters magazine competitions. So far this year she has won a Sanderson duvet cover, a socket set, and a year's supply of Fray Bentos (this explains a lot). She is hoping to win a holiday in Florida with her witty completion of the line 'I love Germoloids haemorrhoid cream because . . . ' She wrote 'it is top for my bottom.' It is surprisingly clever for her.

9 p.m.
In bed. Will lose dark circles by Sunday at this rate.

. . . .

Thursday 4
9 a.m.
Still raining.

1 p.m.
Still raining.

3 p.m.
When will this deluge end? My hair is mass of hideous damp-induced fluff and am likely to go down with

pleurisy or consumption. Although that would be excellent for making Mum regret her hasty decision to send me to stay with the Cleggs. Plus loads of tragic heroines die from consumption like Nicole Kidman in *Moulin Rouge*.

Friday 5

9 a.m.

Still raining. This cannot go on. My hair is the size of a spacehopper. Am going to have to get it cut. Plus the roots are showing. Granny Clegg says I look like a young Myra Hindley. I do not think it is a compliment.

3 p.m.

Granny Clegg has made an appointment for me at Brenda's Hairdressing. It is with Brenda herself. I am hoping she is an innovative style director like Nicky Clarke.

Saturday 6

Brenda is not an innovative style director. She is a forty year old from Penzance with nicotine-stained fingers. She suggested a radical elfin cut to remove the blonde and frizz. I was foolishly swayed by the possibility of looking like vintage Audrey Hepburn and so let her hack at my hair with blunt scissors and a razor for two hours. I do not look like Audrey Hepburn. I look like an eight-year-old boy, i.e. James.

Auntie Joyless is coming for Sunday lunch tomorrow. At least she will approve of my hairdo. I look like a shaven penitent.

. . . .

Sunday 7

My life is not as bad as I thought. Compared to Auntie Joyless my mum is like Julie Cooper-Nichol (except without the porn star past or yacht). Uncle John and my cousins Boaz and Mary are living a life of puritanical misery. They do not even own a television. Oh my God. You'd think they'd at least watch *Songs of Praise*. Boaz smiled at me insanely throughout the meal. He has a weird look in his eye. It is lucky that guns are banned or I fear his repression may lead to a Columbine-style massacre at Redruth High. Auntie Joyless asked if I was repenting my straying from the path of righteousness. Luckily my mouth was full of claggy Smash so I couldn't answer. Then Grandpa Clegg started in on the outrage of changing the name Jif to Cif and how Tony Blair and Brussels were to blame so I escaped further interrogation.

. . . .

Monday 8

Rained. Ate mini Kievs. Read *Of Mice and Men*. We are doing it for GCSE next year. It is not about mice, it is

196

about a giant retard called Lennie. The Kylies are going to have a field day.

Tuesday 9

Stopped raining. Went to Spar with Granny Clegg. Bought Steakhouse Grills and frozen carrots. Came home. Ate them.

Wednesday 10

Got up. Nothing happened. Went to bed. Now I know why Mum left Cornwall the first chance she had. Every day is like Sunday. Without *The O.C.* or Waitrose.

Thursday 11

Mum rang to check on me. I said my life was one long miserable prison sentence. She said, 'Good.' I asked what was happening in Saffron Walden. She said the dog had got stuck in the washing machine, Grandpa had twisted his ankle falling off James's mini trampoline (now banned—she always knew it was a deathtrap), and her mung beans had failed to cultivate. It sounded so exciting I started to cry and begged her to take me back. I reminded her that Redruth is the suicide capital of the UK and that I was severely depressed but she told me not to be so dramatic and that she would see me in two weeks and not to eat the arctic roll in the freezer as it was two years past its sell-by. I will not need to commit suicide anyway. I will die of boredom at this rate.

Friday 12

1 p.m.
Something interesting has happened! People have arrived at the holiday cottage opposite (aka Hester Trelowarren's battery chicken shed). There is a row of green wellies lined up outside the front door and a Range Rover parked outside. More importantly, one of their children looks distinctly like the non-ugly one in Busted. A Waitrose van has delivered their shopping. Grandpa Clegg is all riled up. He says they are taking homes away from natives. I said the only natives they had ousted from their home were chickens but Grandpa said that wasn't the point. Granny Clegg is more concerned as to why they have spurned the supermarket Mecca that is Spar. She is going over to investigate.

3 p.m.
Granny Clegg has returned (an hour and half later). She says they are called Rory and Fiona Britt-Jones and come from Fulham, he is a doctor and she is an interior designer (not a real job, according to Granny Clegg) and they have two children, Will (15—Busted one) and Poppy-Boo (11).

She said they paid £600 for the week. I bet they were sick when she told them 5,000 battery hens were living in their inglenook five months ago.

- -

Saturday 13
Have met Will! The Britt-Jones's came over to thank Granny Clegg for the cake she had left for them (Mr Kipling's French Fancies—she is trying to lure them to Spar). Will is gorgeous. I think I am in love. It is like *Pretty in Pink* (another of Suzy's favourite films) with me as the impoverished but beautiful and vintage Molly Ringwald and him as rich but open-minded Andrew McCarthy. Or like Darcy and Lizzie Bennett. Oh hurrah. Only I am going to have to plan my wardrobe with more care. I fear on first impressions he may have thought I was a celtic inbred. My hair does look marginally asylum-like, plus I had on the enormous, formerly flea-ridden jumper and Granny Clegg's slipper socks.

- -

Sunday 14
Lurked outside in front garden trying to look interesting and beautiful but *Of Mice and Men* got all soggy in the drizzle and then Granny Clegg opened the window and asked if I wanted her to boil wash my underwear as she was doing Grandpa Clegg's. Asked Granny if she had seen the Britt-Joneses and she said they had gone to Eden at

8.30 and wouldn't be back until 7. Why does no one tell me these things? I may have caught pneumonia now. I was only wearing my inside-out T-shirt and the reduced length Monsoon skirt.

Monday 15

Britt-Joneses gone to bloody Tate Gallery in St Ives today. I do not blame them, there is nothing to do in St Slaughter unless you count the fruit machine in the launderette. Plus they probably want to get away from Granny Clegg's incessant questioning. She makes Jeremy Paxman look half-hearted.

Tuesday 16

2 p.m.
I have found my opportunity to bond with Will. Smoking. Granny Clegg says Maureen Penrice from Spar said he bought a packet of Marlboro Lights and a Yorkie this morning. I am going to join him in his illicit habit. Admittedly, I don't know how to smoke but it can't be hard—the Kylies had learned by the age of 10.

8 p.m.
Have just had bonding cigarette moment with Will on the broken swings in the St Slaughter Community Playground (disused). I followed him there after tea (fish

fingers, tinned sweetcorn, Black Forest gateau). I asked if I could 'cadge a fag' (I learnt this from Thin Kylie—she has her uses) and he said, 'Yeah—don't tell the old girl though.' That is his mum. He is so cool. We had a deep and meaningful discussion ('Why are Walker's cheese and onion crisp packets blue when everyone else's are green?' and 'Oompa Loompa out of *Charlie and the Chocolate Factory*—dwarf or midget?') while I wafted the cigarette about. Then he asked if I was going to actually smoke it as he didn't want to waste a good fag so I sucked on it casually like Kylie does but it must have been an extra strong cigarette or something because then I couldn't breathe and started choking and felt totally sick. Will laughed but I think it was with me not at me. At least I hope so, because romance is definitely in the air. We are meeting again tomorrow night.

. . . .

Wednesday 17

I have snogged Will! (First real kiss, unless you count no tongues with Brian Drain on the Year Seven coach trip to Peterborough Roller Rink.) I felt so sick with excitement/fear I was worried I might actually throw up on him like Fat Kylie (actually sick in Dean Auger's mouth at the Wimbish Village Disco, but it was cider not passion that was the cause). We met at the swings again. I did not smoke this time—I said my asthma might flare up. (This is not a total lie—I might have latent asthma.)

Will asked why a girl like me (!) was staying in 'Hicksville, Arizona' and why my hair was so short. I said I had done some 'wild things' and it was all punishment, which he thought was 'way cool, like Joan of Arc'. I did not tell him about the Smints or Brenda. It would ruin the effect. He is my soul mate. He knows all the words to the *O.C.* theme tune. I am going to go to the Witchcraft Museum tomorrow with his mum and dad and Poppy-Boo. It is like a date! I don't think I will be able to sleep.

Thursday 18

Went to the Wicca House with the Britt-Joneses. Fiona and Rory did not seem entirely thrilled at our love for each other but that is what happened to Lizzie Bennett with evil Caroline Bingley and Lady Catherine De Thingy so is only to be expected in across-the-divide love affairs. Poppy-Boo is a brat. She made sick noises when we tried to kiss behind the rune cabinet.

Will is going back to Fulham tomorrow. I said we should meet at 'our place' tonight to say goodbye properly. He asked what 'our place' was. I said the disused playground. He said, 'Right—of course. I was joking.'

10 p.m.

It has happened! I have let Will touch my M&S bra (32AA). He said we are in love so it is OK. I think he wanted to touch more but Maureen Penrice came past with her German shepherd Arnie so we had to stop. I cannot believe he is leaving tomorrow. He has given me his Zippo lighter to remember him by. I will treasure it always.

Friday 19
Will has gone home in his Range Rover. We are going to call each other every day. We will not let distance ruin our relationship like Scarlet and Axe. Or maybe it will be like *Grease* and he will show up at John Major High next term but will have to pretend he doesn't know me because we are too different!

Saturday 20
I am loveless. Tried lying in bed all day moping but Granny Clegg told me to get out because she needed to Shake'n'Vac. I don't know why she bothers. Nothing will get out the ingrained smell of meat pie. I wish Scarlet was still talking to me so I could tell her about Will. Or that I had mobile phone reception to talk to anyone. I may as well be on Mars. I cannot even text Will to tell him I still love him and Granny Clegg won't let me use the BT phone because it is too expensive. This is hypocritical—she wastes pounds ringing up Mum to whitter on about nothing.

7 p.m.
Hope is in sight. We are going to Auntie Joyless's house for lunch tomorrow. They live near a giant satellite dish so there is bound to be mobile reception.

- -

Sunday 21

Hurrah—there is mobile reception in Goonglaze Road. But it was a double-edged sword. Auntie Joyless confiscated my phone after it beeped during our puritanical lunch (boiled ham and potatoes, apples for pudding). Then, when I finally got my phone back, the text was not from Will at all but from Sad Ed to say Happy Birthday (he sent it two weeks ago). Scarlet is losing her Grace-like grip. Or, more probably, she has gone away.

Boaz offered to 'come and play' tomorrow. Auntie Joyless did not look pleased but Boaz said he would bring his Noah's ark and Creationism quiz book so she has reluctantly agreed. I wish she hadn't. I do not want to be seen with a boy who wears sandals and socks.

- -

Monday 22

Boaz came over. The Creationism thing was a cover-up. He wanted to quiz me about my stand against repression. He says he is thinking of upping his resistance to Auntie Joyless and that I am his role model. He asked if he can come to live in Saffron Walden. I have warned him that there is no Ribena and that Grandpa Riley is doing some very unbiblical things but he said he didn't care and would I ask my mum.

5 p.m.
Oh my God. I have got my period! Maybe Boaz has weird religious powers like Reverend Billy and his verruca-healing hands. I am going to Spar immediately. I cannot tell Granny Clegg.

6 p.m.
Am wearing giant Spar own-brand sanitary towels. It is like having a nappy on. I rustle when I walk.

7 p.m.
Granny Clegg has rung Mum to tell her I have 'the curse'. I thought it might be the rustling that gave it away but apparently Maureen Penrice told Hester who told her that I had bought 'sanitary provisions'. Is nothing sacred?

I told Mum about Boaz and she said it was just a 'phase' and not to worry. I am worried. He wears 'Jesus Loves Me' T-shirts. I will be the social equivalent of Emily Reeve. Good God, if anyone needed mobile phone reception it is now. I am going to walk to Redruth if I have to tomorrow so that I can phone Sad Ed. Only he will understand my plight. Plus Will must have called by now.

Tuesday 23

Did not have to walk to Redruth. It turns out you can get two bars on the top of the disused climbing frame. I called Sad Ed and he confessed that Scarlet has been brainwashing him but that he cannot afford to lose her friendship in case I am exiled for good, plus she is a good source of illegally downloaded music and sex advice (both via Suzy). He said we could meet in secret when I get home. Then I told him about Will and my torrid holiday romance and he went quiet, so I asked him how his life was and he said it was like living inside the lyrics of 'Teenage Dirtbag'. I do not know how, he doesn't know any girls called Noelle, or like Iron Maiden. Then the phone went dead. It must be the poor quality reception. I may write to Orange to complain about the transmitter situation in rural areas.

No call from Will yet. Maybe his parents have forbidden him to call me and are forcing him to go out with someone called Tiffany whose dad owns a Porsche and who does not have a wonky hairdo.

8 p.m.

I do not see what the period fuss is all about. It is all highly uncomfortable and undignified. I am not leaping for joy or wearing tight white clothing like in the adverts. I am wearing giant pants and Granny Clegg is making me eat liver once a day to replace lost iron. It is torture.

Wednesday 24

Went to the climbing frame again and called Will. He sounded weird. I asked why he hadn't called and he said he was in trouble because his mum had found out about him smoking (Maureen Penrice) and in the heat of the moment he had said it was my influence. I asked him if he still loved me but then the beeps went and my credit ran out. Went to the Spar to top it up but it shuts at one on a Wednesday due to the cattle market 'in the big town'.

Thursday 25

Called Will again. He said I should stop wasting my minutes on him but I said love was never a waste. Then I heard someone giggling in the background. I demanded to know who it was and he said it was Poppy-Boo but then there were kissing noises and he said he had to go as an emergency had come up.

Friday 26

I am single again. I called Will and told him that I knew about him and Tiffany. He said, 'Who's Tiffany?' and I said she was metaphorical and might be called Tara for all I knew but that wasn't the point. He said, 'What is the point?' and I said that I didn't think he believed in me any more and that I couldn't believe in someone who didn't believe in me, and he said, 'What the f**k are you on about?' Admittedly the line was stolen directly from *Pretty in Pink* when Andrew McCarthy is too embarrassed to admit he doesn't want to take Molly Ringwald to the prom but it totally fitted our situation. So I said 'It's over,' and he said, 'It never began,' and we hung up. It was utterly Julie Burchill. I am devastated. I will never love again.

Saturday 27

Granny Clegg is ecstatic. She has won the holiday in Florida. They are going in October. The makers of Germoloids must have been short of entries. I tried to be happy for them but I am still mourning Will so I smiled and then went back to sighing by the window and reading *The Bell Jar*. Granny Clegg said she is glad Dad is picking me up on Monday. She says it is worse than when Auntie Joyless found out that Jesus had died for her sins and would not come out of her room for a week.

Boaz is coming over tomorrow to say goodbye. I have begged Granny and Grandpa not to go out but Granny says she is not missing the St Slaughter giant vegetable competition for the world.

Sunday 28

Boaz has just gone. He has agreed to try to convert the forces of repression (i.e. Auntie Joyless) from within.

Thank God. My fragile reputation is safe. I told him to be careful—being a rebel youth wasn't as easy as it looked—but he went all biblical and said it was like Revelation and Judgement Day. Then he asked if he could have my Sienna Miller scarf as a symbol of our joint struggle against authority. I let him. It is quite flattering to have a minion. He tied it round his head and asked me to wish him luck. I did. He will need it.

Monday 29
Late Summer Bank Holiday (UK)
2 p.m.
Dad is here. He is eating Viennetta in the garden with Granny and Grandpa and the dog. Grandpa allowed it to come on the grounds that Dad is not to let it out of his sight for a second—not even to go to the toilet. Dad says something has happened at home but that he can't tell me in front of Granny and Grandpa Clegg. Maybe Mum has had a kind of conversion and has gone all permissive. Or maybe she has a terminal illness. I could donate my bone marrow and nearly die on the operating table. They could turn it into a film.

10 p.m.
Am back in civilization—i.e. Saffron Walden. I still do not know what has happened. Mum said I was too weak from travelling to cope and that she would tell me in the

209

morning. James was in bed so I couldn't quiz him. He is easily bribed.

. . . .

Tuesday 30

Oh my God. No one is dying. It is worse. Treena isn't bulimic. She is five months pregnant and Grandpa is the father. They are going to keep it. I am going to have an uncle or aunt who is fourteen years younger than me. I am white trash. No wonder Will spurned me.

Also, a hurricane has flooded America. James said it is retribution for George Bush's invasion of Iraq. I said I didn't think God was on the side of Saddam Hussein but James said it was nothing to do with God—it was Allah. Mum went a bit pale. I think she is worried Mumtaz is converting him to Islam.

Granny Clegg rang in a panic. Their resort in Florida has been partially submerged. Mum said it was a good thing and wouldn't they be better off in Newquay anyway, but Granny Clegg said a bit of rain and wind never put her off. She is determined to be the first person from St Slaughter to go to America.

. . . .

Wednesday 31

Called Sad Ed to tell him about Grandpa and Treena. He agrees it is shocking. Asked him to come over later but he is going to Scarlet's to help with their Hurricane Katrina

210

Appeal. I said I would help as well but he said it was not advisable as Scarlet was still not talking to me. I said that I was no longer consorting with the Kylies (this is true—I haven't seen them yet—they are probably in America getting flooded) and he said he would put in a good word for me. I will win her back once school starts. She will be bored in maths without me.

Thursday 1

Mum has found Will's Zippo. I explained it wasn't mine but she has confiscated it anyway and done a forensic search of my bedroom for smoking evidence (findings— nil). Mum said I will be sent to live with Granny Clegg permanently if my poor behaviour goes on.

Friday 2

Granny Clegg rang. Auntie Joyless has had a minor breakdown. She got back from a prayer group meeting at the Farmers' Union hall and found Boaz 'reading the devil's literature' (i.e. *FHM* magazine) and 'wearing women's clothing' (i.e. my Sienna Miller scarf). Uncle John has called in Father Abraham (I am not joking) from their extremist church to perform an exorcism. It is all my fault. I hope he does not grass me up to Auntie Joyless.

Saturday 3

Treena came over. She is gigantic. I hope it is not twins. She let James put his hands on her tummy and feel the kicking. Mum looked horrified. She asked if they had told Treena's husband Des about the impending arrival yet. Treena said he was in solitary confinement for a week for headbutting the prison cook but that she was going on Thursday to break the news. She said she was going to have a civilized grown-up discussion and ask for a divorce

215

and the house. I do not think Des will give her either of these things. By all accounts he is neither civilized nor grown-up. They had better sort it out soon though. He is due to be released into the community with his electronic tag in a month.

Sunday 4

Thin Kylie is not coming back to school tomorrow (she came over to show off her Corfu-acquired tan). She says Cherie is worried that I might be a bad influence on her. That is a joke. Kylie is the worst influence in John Major High. She is going to St Gregory's Girls instead. I asked how she got in (they have a rigorous entrance exam and a catchment area of three roads) and she said Terry has paid for a new roof for the needlework wing. Even the nuns are corrupt these days. I blame the New Labour era of sleaze. Kylie is gutted about the uniform though. It is brown with a straw hat. Not even she can make that look sluttish.

Monday 5

8 a.m.

I take it back. Have just seen Thin Kylie getting into the 4x4 in her school uniform. The brown skirt is halfway up her thighs and her white shirt is undone revealing a black Wonderbra. Even the hat manages to look like something

216

in one of Mark Lambert's magazines. I am glad she is going. I predict I will be able to win Scarlet back by first break.

4 p.m.
Scarlet is still sulking. Although according to Sad Ed she did say that my hair looked avant-garde. She is weakening.

On the plus side, Mrs Brain's fast food menu has been ousted and the school canteen has gone totally Jamie Oliver (Scarlet is triumphant—her hummus sandwich rally has finally been called off). There was a near riot at lunchtime though when Fat Kylie was offered a choice of pitta pockets or foccacia. She said, 'Don't you f**king swear at me, where's my f**king pizza?' Mrs Brain called Mr Wilmott and demanded a return to 'traditional cooking' (i.e. microwaving nuggets) but he said he was under orders from the LEA and that someone from the Government was coming to visit the school next week as it is a model healthy eating establishment so there was no way chips were going back on the menu before then. The crisp and Coke machine was sold out in a record fifteen minutes.

I hope it is not so-called 'Blair Babe' Education Secretary Ruth Kelly who is coming to visit. She has the voice of a man and the hair of a lunatic. She should get some pointers from Suzy who is living proof you can be politically minded and dress like a high-class prostitute.

Tuesday 6

The Jamie Oliver menu is still not the roaring success Mr Wilmott was hoping for. Lessons started fifteen minutes late this afternoon due to the queues of Year Tens at Mr Patel's waiting for microwave Ginsters.

Wednesday 7

I have found a way to get back in with Scarlet. She and Jack have joined the drama club (they are going to lobby for the *Rocky Horror Show* as their next production). I am going to sign up immediately. It means I get off games. Plus being an actress would be totally glamorous and ethereal. I may very well become the next Kate Winslet. I asked Sad Ed if he would join as well (I need back-up) and he has agreed as long as he doesn't have to wear skimpy underwear on stage (he is still several pounds over his target weight).

Thursday 8

Treena has been to see Des. It did not go according to plan. There was a fight during which they both had to be restrained. Des is now back in solitary and his parole has been put back until December.

Grandpa is going to move in to Treena's semi on the Whiteshot Estate. Treena says she is not ashamed of her generation gap love any more. James said she should be but Treena did not hear him—she was too busy eating Wotsits for two.

Friday 9

Saw Jack on C corridor at break. He asked how Cornwall was. I said I was fully reformed. He said that was a shame. I asked if Scarlet had mentioned me at all and he said only in the same sentence as the words cow and loser. I can see she is not going to be broken easily.

Saturday 10

Grandpa has moved out. I think Mum was actually sad to see him go. He was a source of constant spillage for her so she will have nothing to do in the day now. Although it may have been disappointment that the dog is staying. Treena has refused to take it—she says it is a health hazard to the baby. This is rich coming from someone who owns a budgie called Christina (as in Aguilera) who is allowed to poo freely on the sofa.

Sunday 11

10 a.m.

Scarlet has rung. She is coming over this afternoon to discuss our relationship. Suzy and Sad Ed have worn her down. Hurrah. We will be reunited and I can tell her about the tragedy of Will. Plus I will have someone to borrow clothes off again.

5 p.m.
The reunion did not go according to plan. Thin Kylie showed up with a bottle of Thunderbird and *Hot Celebrities* and Scarlet went all scary and said I had to make a choice between the 'chavs and the chav-nots'. So Kylie said, 'I ain't no f**kin' chav, Dracula, and anyway, she'll choose me, cos I got a swimming pool, innit,' and sat down on the bed. This is not true. I would choose Scarlet over her any day, but I was worried about repercussions from Kylie so I kept quiet. But Scarlet looked at me with her cat-like eyes (she has inherited that gift from Suzy) and said, 'Your silence speaks volumes,' and swept out of the room in her new goth coat (vegetarian leather). Then Thin Kylie said she had to go anyway as she had Latin homework.

I rang Sad Ed and he agreed this is a major setback. He does not see much hope of a reunion before Christmas.

Monday 12
Mr Patel has installed a Pot Noodle stop in his newsagents (i.e. a machine that boils water and a fork dispenser). I am full of admiration for his entrepreneurship—he will be able to fully exploit the gap in the market for E-number-laden junk food now that Mrs Brain has gone organic.

Tuesday 13

Grandpa came over for tea. He says he wanted to see the dog but I think he misses Mum's cooking as well. Treena just eats Lean Cuisine and crisps. He said the Whiteshot Estate is not that bad if you ignore the constant roar of minibikes and the smell of convenience food. Mum asked if they had come up with any names yet. He said Treena wants to call it Harvey. Mum said what about if it's a girl and Grandpa said, 'That too.' This is not good. Treena's surname is Nichols.

Wednesday 14

Went to my first drama club meeting. It is a disparate group of eager theatre freaks (Jack, Scarlet, me, Sad Ed) and not so eager Retards and Criminals who are forced to do it as part of their rehab (Davey 'flasher' MacDonald and Jason Kinsey). Justin Statham and Sophie Jacobs are in it as well (they are neither nerds nor retards but a third way of beautiful people). Mr Vaughan is in charge. It is part of his teacher training. He says we can vote on the new production, as part of his democratic teaching method. I have voted for *Hamlet*. Sad Ed asked if we could do a musical version of the life of Jim Morrison, featuring songs by The Doors, but Scarlet told him to shut up and made him vote for *Rocky Horror*.

It is not Ruth Kelly who is visiting the school. It is Prime Minister Tony Blair. Sad Ed says Scarlet says Suzy is in overdrive and is planning to infiltrate the school so that she can meet him. I do not think she will succeed. Mr Wilmott and Suzy have a history of not seeing eye to eye.

Thursday 15

There has been mass Pot Noodle injury due to Mr Patel's introduction of a chilli variety. Mrs Leech was in overdrive administering ice packs and soothing cans of Sprite. Mr Wilmott looked worried. Tony Blair is coming tomorrow and the canteen is conspicuously quiet these days.

Friday 16

10 a.m.

The school is crawling with security guards ahead of Tony Blair's visit. There was a mild panic in the sixth form common room when sniffer dogs showed up but it turns out that these ones can only smell bombs not drugs. Mr Wilmott has planned ahead quite well—the Retards and Criminals are on a day visit to a fishfinger factory and Mrs Brain is on annual leave. (Ms Hopwood-White has reluctantly agreed to pose as a go-getting dinner lady instead.)

4 p.m.

Tony Blair's visit was not the resounding success hoped for. Plans were going well. Mr Wilmott had managed to lure people away from Mr Patel's with a carrot and stick approach (a temporary 'no leaving the school at lunchtime' rule and a promise to reinstate doughnuts by Monday) so that by 12.15 everyone was eating broccoli and sipping spring water but then Suzy, who had managed to evade school security (i.e. Mrs Leech) by coming through the gap in the sheep-field fence, threw herself at Tony Blair outside the mobile science labs in an act of comradeship (according to Suzy), and potential terrorism (according to the Secret Service). Tony Blair got bundled back into his blacked-out Rover before he could sample the three-bean pilaff and Suzy got arrested.

I do not know what Suzy sees in him anyway. His teeth are sinister.

Saturday 17

Grandpa and Treena are getting married. They came round after *CD:UK* to share the happy news. Mum is in shock. I think she was hoping Grandpa would come to his senses and grow old gracefully. How he is going to do that with a toddler called Harvey I do not know. Although at least it ends the Nichols threat—Treena is going to change her name to Riley. Dad pointed out that she was still married to a convicted criminal, but Treena said she had already filed for divorce on grounds of mental cruelty. James said, 'Mental illness more like.' So Mum sent him to his room to tidy up his hobbit shrine. I am not sure if

I am happy or not. On the one hand, I am all for controversial love across class, race, and age boundaries but, on the other hand, this is the sort of story that gets featured in *Chat* magazine for £50.

. . . .

Sunday 18

Saw Thin Kylie on the wall. She says St Gregory's is excellent. She has a new best friend called Aaliyah who is fifteen and has a black dad and has done it with three different boys including Mr Whippy, the ice cream man. (aka seventeen-year-old Dave Tennick who got thrown out of John Major High last year for joyriding in Mr Wilmott's Vauxhall Cavalier. At least he is putting his driving skills to good use now.) Why can't I go to a Catholic girls' school instead of a mixed comprehensive. It is so much edgier.

. . . .

Monday 19

James has won the Saffron Walden under-tens literary competition with his story 'Murder Round The Bend'. It is about a man who walks around a corner and gets stabbed to death. The judges said it shows real promise and a flair for minimalist surrealism. I have serious doubts about the judges' credentials. I do not think Mr Goddard the butcher should be involved in discussions on literary merit. He cleaves entire pigs in two for a living.

. . . .

Tuesday 20

It is drama club tomorrow. I hope *Hamlet* wins. I would make an excellent Ophelia. I already know what drowning in a meringue dress feels like.

Wednesday 21

We are not doing *Hamlet*. According to Mr Vaughan it only got one vote. We are doing *Bugsy Malone*, which won by a massive ten votes (the Criminals and Retards discovered it involved guns). Sophie Jacobs is jubilant. She wants to be Tallulah. Auditions are next week. I am going to try for Blousey Brown, innocent but talented new girl in town. She gets to kiss Bugsy (which is bound to be Justin Statham as he is the best looking by far, plus his dad can get programmes printed cheaply). Sad Ed is in a panic. There is a character called Fat Sam and he is worried about typecasting. Scarlet is sulking. She says *Bugsy Malone* is, at best, pro-American propaganda and, at worst, a paedophile's dream come true. I do not know what she thinks *Rocky Horror* would be. It involves gay sex and suspender belts.

Thursday 22

I have learnt all the words to Blousey Brown's song ('Ordinary Fool'—how appropriate). I am going to get the part for sure. I sound almost like Katie Melua.

Friday 23

Saw Justin in B corridor at lunchtime with Jack. With our new-found bond as drama club members I decided to talk to him and said he would make an excellent Bugsy. But then Sophie Jacobs sashayed up singing 'My Name is Tallulah' and whisked him for practice. Jack rolled his eyes and said they deserved each other. How can he speak ill of Justin? Or maybe he was being nice about Sophie. Whichever, he is wrong. Justin deserves me. I am so over Will. He was a rebound boyfriend. Justin is my true destiny.

Saturday 24

Watched *Bugsy Malone* on DVD with James to get tips for my audition. James said Scarlet is right—the film glorifies sex and violence, and is not suitable for a school production. I pointed out that 'Murder Round the Bend' glorified violence but he claims it has an anti-knives subplot.

Sunday 25

Grandpa and Treena came over. Des is contesting her mental cruelty divorce and has filed for divorce himself on grounds of adultery. Treena says she will not give him the satisfaction. I said what did it matter if the end result was the same but Treena said it was a matter of pride. But she is adulterous. The proof is due in less than three months.

Monday 26

Rehearsed with Sad Ed after school (Scarlet had to go to Mrs Wong's for a filling and so couldn't intervene to stop us). He said I was excellent, but that my husky voice sounded a bit more menacing than sexy at times. Sad Ed is going to sing Tallulah's song. He says that is the sort of subversive thing Jim Morrison would have done. He is so gay. I was right all along! Hurrah.

Tuesday 27

Scarlet is off school. Jack told Ms Hopwood-White she lost a lot of blood after her filling. I should think she is thrilled. She will look anaemic now, which is the preferred goth skin tone.

Auditions are tomorrow. I actually feel sick. I may have been hasty in likening my singing voice to Katie Melua. The dog howls when I practise.

Wednesday 28

Auditions did not go brilliantly. Mr Vaughan had decided to do them *X-Factor* style with Ms Hopwood-White as Sharon Osbourne. Three Year Eights left in tears. I got off mildly. He said my voice was interestingly unpolished. I think that might be good. Ms Hopwood-White said it was a 'Yes' from her. Sad Ed is through as well. Mr Vaughan said his rendition of 'My Name is Tallulah' was hilarious. Although I am not sure that is the effect Ed was aiming for.

Thursday 29

Saw Mr Vaughan outside the mobile science lab having a cigarette. I asked him if he had made his decision on Blousey Brown yet. He said there was only one girl for the part. Yes, but which one?

Sad Ed has invited me to his birthday party on Saturday. He is going to make vodka martinis and play lounge music. I asked him if Scarlet was going. He said no.

Friday 30

Went into town to find Sad Ed a birthday present. Got him ten Flyte bars and *Will and Grace* Season One on DVD (on offer in WHSmith for £6.99, purchased when Mrs Noakes safely on lunchbreak).

October

Saturday 1

Sad Ed lied. Scarlet was at his birthday party. She was not pleased to see me—apparently he had lied to her about my presence as well. Plus there were no vodka martinis or lounge music. Mrs Thomas served jelly and devilled eggs and made us play musical chairs to 'Walking in the Air' until Scarlet claimed I had cheated by using an orthopaedic footstool as a chair and refused to join in until I was sent off. It was all over by 7 so I went home and ate the contents of my party bag (except the miniature playing cards, obviously) and watched *Casualty*. I would make an excellent paramedic. I am decisive and compassionate, plus I love tragedy and look good in green.

Sunday 2

Granny Clegg called. Father Abraham's exorcism has worked. Boaz is back singing 'The Battle Hymn of the Republic' and wearing boys' clothes (Clark's shoes and tank tops). What is wrong with the men in our family? They all give in at the first sign of torture or bribery.

Monday 3

Sad Ed thanked me for the presents. Flyte bars are key to his weight loss programme. He has eaten three today already. I asked him if he had watched any *Will and Grace* yet but he said that all the discs had a bite-sized chunk out of them and were unplayable. (Aaagh—dog must have got to it after I watched several episodes—just to check quality, of course.)

Tuesday 4

Jewish New Year
First day of Ramadan

Mum is not pleased. James is on a fast in religious sympathy with Islam. He can only eat during hours of darkness, which has messed up her strict meal and bed timetable. He will not last the week. Plus I doubt Reverend Begley will have any sympathy with his embracing of world religions.

Wednesday 5

I am not Blousey. Sophie Microwave Muffins Jacobs got the part. She is neither innocent, nor talented. I bet her dad is providing catering. The casting is all over the place. Oona Rickets is Tallulah. Jack is Bugsy. Justin is Dandy Dan. Scarlet is a man. I am a chorus dancer. So is Fat Kylie (I pity Mrs Mathias's needlework class making her costume). Worst of all I have to slow dance with black cleaner-cum-tap-legend Fizzy (Davey MacDonald—neither black nor able to dance, to my knowledge). The only appropriate casting is Sad Ed as Fat Sam. So his

232

subversive and gay tendencies did not pay off. Rehearsals get under way next week. Mr Vaughan is instigating an experimental and democratic teaching method—people can choose not to come to rehearsals. He is hoping it will instil a sense of responsibility and teamwork amongst the cast. I won't hold my breath.

. . . .

Thursday 6

James's Ramadan fast has ended. He went dizzy during netball (non-sexist sports coaching) and had to be force-fed chocolate milk to revive him. He is going to pray to Mecca five times a day instead. I asked where hobbits featured in Islam's teachings. He said this was typical of such a small-minded Westerner and that Islam was not the exclusive, extremist religion it was cracked up to be.

. . . .

Friday 7

James's praying to Mecca has ended. He says it interferes with CBBC too much. Plus the dog got overexcited and chewed his prayer mat (an M&S beach towel).

. . . .

Saturday 8

Went to see Grandpa Riley and Treena. They are living in semi-squalor. There were biscuit wrappers and budgie poo all over the floor. Grandpa says it is because neither he nor Treena can bend down any more due to lumbago and heavy pregnancy respectively. I felt sorry for Grandpa, he is not used to council estate conditions, so I hoovered up and washed the dishes for them. I drew the line at cleaning out the loo though. I know how much time Treena spent with her head down it.

Sunday 9

Granny Clegg called to say goodbye. She and Grandpa Clegg are off to Florida tomorrow. She told Mum her will was in the bread bin. They have never been on a plane before and are convinced it will be hijacked or flown into a tall building by Osama Bin Laden. Mum said it wasn't too late to cancel the trip (she is worried about Dad having to fly out to rescue them from a situation) but Granny Clegg said no beardy-weirdy is going to stop her from seeing one of the seven wonders of the world. Mum said she wasn't aware of a wonder in Florida and Granny Clegg said they were thinking of a day trip to the Grand Canyon. Mum went all pale. The Grand Canyon is 2,570 miles from Florida (James googled it). The possibilities for disaster are endless.

Auntie Joyless is driving them to Gatwick. At least there is no chance of getting lost on that stage of the journey.

Monday 10

The flight was not from Gatwick. It was from Heathrow. Luckily they had left eight hours check in and sightseeing time (the airport is a wonder of the world in itself to Granny Clegg) so Auntie Joyless managed to get the Metro round the M25 to Terminal 3 with four hours to spare. The plane has taken off and there are no reports of incidents involving midget pensioners. Mum checked on Ceefax and rang the airline.

Tuesday 11

The provisional SAT results are out. John Major High is at the bottom of the league, beating only the Sharon Davies Special School in Braintree. Mr Wilmott gave a talk in Assembly. He said we had let the school down.

Wednesday 12

Mr Vaughan is being forced to rethink his democratic teaching method. Dandy Dan's and Fat Sam's gangs (i.e. Davey MacDonald and the rest of the Criminals and Retards) did not show up for group rehearsal—they were behind the mobile science lab, smoking. Mr Wilmott found them and returned them to the drama room with a withering look. Then we tried the opening dance routine (as choreographed by Sophie Jacobs) but it got stopped after a fight between the gangs broke out behind the wardrobe department (aka a wardrobe). Jason Kinsey said they were just getting into character so Mr Vaughan suggested their gang leaders (aka Sad Ed and Justin) start using their leadership skills but Jason said he wasn't taking orders from a 'fat bender'. Mr Vaughan has decided to schedule separate rehearsals until the gangs can channel their ASBO tendencies into their performance.

I have individual rehearsal with Davey MacDonald tomorrow. I hope his special needs do not evidence themselves.

Thursday 13

Oh my God. Davey MacDonald can dance. I was right all along. He does have special skills alongside his perverted habits. Mr Vaughan is beside himself. He thinks he has discovered Billy Elliot. He is going to phone the Royal Ballet. Davey MacDonald did not look keen but Mr Vaughan said that he would get to wear tights, which are extremely revealing. Maybe I was too hasty in dismissing Davey as a thick pervert. Ballet dancers are all deep and meaningful and have eccentric eating disorders and things. *Très* romantic.

Friday 14

A postcard arrived from Granny Clegg. It was from Heathrow Airport. It said:

Having a lovely time. Have tried foreign food already at a restaurant called McDonalds—have you heard of it? Apparently it is very popular in America. Love to Valerie.

PS. Call Hester and tell her she can have the arctic roll in the freezer. I think it may be past its best.

Saturday 15

Grandpa has asked if I will be his bridesmaid at his forthcoming wedding. I said that technically, the wedding was not really forthcoming as Treena's divorce wasn't settled yet but he said that was a mere detail. I hope he is not thinking of becoming a bigamist. It would be all over GMTV with pictures of me in my compost-stained bridesmaid's dress. Maybe I can get a new and cool dress. I will ask Mum. I could be an excellent vintage bridesmaid.

5 p.m.

Mum says she is not wasting money on trips to London to buy vintage Chanel. She says she will try Vanish

Oxy-Action on the compost dress or I can make do with my school uniform skirt and one of her blouses. Shudder.

Sunday 16

Went round Sad Ed's. Scarlet was there. It was a strained hour and a half. She and Ed are going to London at half term to buy goth clothes and man make-up. I casually suggested we could visit Old Compton Street (famous gay road in London and ideal territory to gauge Sad Ed's Will factor). Scarlet snorted and said Bob and Suzy were driving them and there wouldn't be room for me. That is not true. Volvos are notoriously spacious and, anyway, I could sit in the boot.

Monday 17

8 p.m.

Grandpa Clegg is missing in a theme park. Granny Clegg reversed charges from her motel room. He was last seen two hours ago walking towards the *Back to the Future* ride in a state of 'shock and awe'. She wants Dad to fly out to help her hunt for him. Dad has refused. He says he has an important meeting on Thursday to discuss his work's photocopier servicing contract. Mum told Granny to call the police but Granny said she wasn't trusting her husband's life to someone called Chip or Brad.

1 a.m.

Granny Clegg has just called (reversed charges again)—
Grandpa Clegg has been found alive. He had come over
funny in a tunnel and had to be taken to the emergency
medical and lost children room. Dad is relieved. The
future of his photocopier contract is safe.

Tuesday 18

Granny Clegg has called again. This time to ask what grits
are. Mum has banned reverse charge phone calls except
in matters of life or death.

Wednesday 19

Thank God I am doing excellent drama instead of hockey
with the lesbians. According to Mrs Leech, there were
four electrocutions, a missing front tooth, and a possible
pneumonia today. I am amazed school sport has not
been banned. Statistically, it is more dangerous than
Formula One.

Thursday 20

Mum has gone bird flu mad. She has taken down
the half coconuts and blue-tit box and done a cursory
sweep of the neighbourhood for diseased pigeons
etc. (findings—one suspicious sparrow in Marjory's

Leylandii). Duck feeding is out, as is tonight's planned Coq Au Vin.

- -

Friday 21

Mum's paranoia knows no bounds. She has broken her self-imposed long distance phone call rules to get Granny Clegg to bring back some Tamiflu in case we get infected by a rogue pigeon. They were out at a line dancing competition though so she had to leave a message with someone called Randy.

- -

Saturday 22

Thin Kylie came over today with her new friend Aaliyah. Her dad is an Ambassador and her mum is an ex-supermodel. This explains the errant behaviour. Thin Kylie had told her about my morning-after pill services and she asked if she could get some as Mr Whippy wasn't keen on condoms. I said that the morning-after pill was not a method of contraception and Thin Kylie said, 'But it, like, stops you getting up the spout, so, like, of course it is.' So I suggested she went on the pill instead and that Dr Braithwaite was usually happy to oblige.

4 p.m.

Oh God. What if Aaliyah tells Dr Braithwaite it was me

who suggested she went on the pill. Mum is bound to start a campaign to get the age of consent raised.

. . . .

Sunday 23

Granny and Grandpa Clegg have been arrested for drug smuggling at Heathrow. The Tamiflu turned out to be Temazepam—a prescription sedative apparently favoured by hardcore drug addicts and celebrities. Granny Clegg says she is sure that is the message she got from the bellboy Randy, who kindly got her the drugs. Dad is driving down there now to sort it out.

Mum is more concerned about her lack of bird flu antidote. She is refusing to visit Grandpa Riley until Christina has been given the all clear.

11 p.m.

Dad is back. Granny and Grandpa Clegg are free. Dad pointed out their inherent stupidity and thus inability to mastermind an international drugs ring and the police reluctantly agreed. They have been let off with a fine for importing restricted goods instead.

. . . .

Monday 24

It is half term. Once again I am friendless (Sad Ed is getting ready for his trip to London with Scarlet tomorrow. They are planning their 'looks' with military precision.) and being forced to take solace in literature.

I am reading *Down and Out in Paris and London*. I wish I was.

. . . .

Tuesday 25

It is not fair. Sad Ed and Scarlet are in London while I am languishing in the middle-class backwater that is North Essex. I could be brushing shoulders with Sienna and Kate while we scour Portobello for unique vintage finds, instead of being forced to go to DeBarrs for new school shoes (Clark's, if previous visits are anything to go by).

3 p.m.

Have new school shoes. They are black Kickers and were hard won after an hour-long battle with Mum, who was veering towards some totally orthopaedic looking Start Rite. Mum agreed on the grounds they had nicely ridged soles, no heels, and good ankle support. Kickers are very retro, which is like vintage only cleaner. Who needs London?

. . . .

Wednesday 26

Saffron Walden is not a shopping Mecca. I was temporarily blinded by DeBarr's experimental footwear stand. Sad Ed got a vintage Crombie (i.e. a dead man's coat) and a skateboard (impulse buy—he will never use

242

it). Plus, he and Scarlet had lunch in the Topshop café next to the fat one out of Blue and Ulrika Johnson (not together—or they could have called *Hello* and made some money). I asked Ed if he had gone to Old Compton Street but he said no, they were too busy buying vegetarian shoes in Covent Garden. Am going to have to find another way to get Sad Ed to come out. Maybe I will rent a Judy Garland DVD and invite Ed over. She is a gay icon. If he agrees to come and see it then I will know for sure.

Thursday 27

Got out *The Wizard of Oz* from BJ Video (aka Blow Job Video). Invited Sad Ed over but he was watching a *Buffy* marathon on Sky. So it is not a total rejection of gay lifestyle, which is promising.

Watched the DVD with James and the dog. Gay men have weird tastes in films. The dog got excited at the little people and ate the box. So now I will have a fine at Blow Job Video.

Friday 28

Oh my God. Thin Kylie is coming back to school on Monday. Mum bumped into Cherie in the bleach section at Waitrose (Cherie had taken a wrong turn in Doritos). Apparently posh Catholic girls are worse than Whiteshot chavs for drug and alcohol abuse and Cherie has taken her out before she is led astray. I should think Terry is gutted he signed that cheque now. I bet the nuns don't do refunds.

. . . .

Saturday 29

Saw Kylie on the front wall. Cherie is a liar. Kylie has been expelled for a list of misdemeanours including refusing to wear regulation pants, sexually provoking the caretaker, and threatening Sister Ignatia with a gel pen. Although Cherie was right about the alcohol. Kylie says Vodka Slammers are de rigeur lunchtime drinking.

. . . .

Sunday 30

British Summer Time ends

James has written to Nestlé. His afternoon KitKat was solid chocolate. You would think that would be a bonus but he is very particular about his chocolate/wafer ratio.

. . . .

Monday 31

Fat Kylie and Thin Kylie are back and are harder than ever. They buried a Year Eight in the high jump pit (aka school cat toilet) at first break just so word got out that they were in charge again. Mr Wilmott did not look thrilled to see Thin Kylie back. Nor did Ms Hopwood-White. She has been enjoying a period of relative authority.

James is out trick or treating. He is dressed (surprise, surprise) as a hobbit. The dog is dressed as a werewolf (no disguise needed). Mum has gone with them. I said I was too old for such childish nonsense.

8.30 p.m.
Why, oh why, did I not go trick or treating? James got eighteen mini Mars bars, a Swizzels selection pack, a Terry's Chocolate Orange and £21.40 in cash. He has counted it five times.

november

24h

ASBO

CUSTARD

Tuesday 1

All Saints Day

Mum has got a new campaign. She is leading the protest against the 24-hour licensing laws due to come in in three weeks. I said she was leaving it a bit late as the law was already passed but she said she hoped to influence money-crazy pub owners into submission.

Wednesday 2

Blind but brilliant David Blunkett has resigned. Again. It is the dog I feel sorry for. It is used to a charmed life. Now it will have to go back to Sheffield and eat Pal and listen to *The Archers* like lesser dogs do.

Rehearsals started again today. Mr Vaughan unveiled the prototype splurge gun, as designed by Mr Potter's Year Ten CDT class. It has been sent back to the drawing board after it backfired and showered Mr Vaughan with Bird's custard.

Thursday 3

Eid Al-Fittr

Grandpa and Treena came over for tea. (James was at Mumtaz's celebrating the end of Ramadan.) There is still no sign of divorce progress. Des says he will make her life a misery if she does not bow to his demands (he wants the house, the black ash coffee table, the Argos sofa, the

Jean-Claude Van Damme DVD collection and the removal of Christina).

Friday 4

Mark Lambert is back. Chavs' corner is complete once more. He said spinning Waltzers wasn't all it was cracked up to be. What was he expecting? The Kylies are a bit fractious though. They have not decided who is going to shag him yet.

Saturday 5

Guy Fawkes Night

Went to the annual Round Table firework display at Caton's Lane, home of Saffron Walden FC (Vicks Inhaler league). Mum did not go—Dad is an official firework lighter and she is scared of seeing him burnt alive by a rogue Catherine wheel. She and the dog watched *Casualty* on loud to block out the noise. Scarlet was there with Bob, Suzy, and Jack. Jack waved and mouthed something but I couldn't hear due to the shrieking of eight year olds in my ears. Scarlet ignored me. She is dragging this out longer than I anticipated.

12 midnight

Cannot sleep. The dog is whimpering under my bed due to the continuing sound of fireworks and outdoor karaoke coming from the Britchers'. Mum has put in her ear plugs. She bought them the day the Britchers arrived 'just in case'.

Sunday 6
The Britchers are still in the garden. It is a scene of lottery winning carnage. From my bedroom (with James's binoculars) I can clearly see a naked man in their pool and several discarded Asti Spumante bottles. They are probably getting into practice for 24-hour drinking. Mum has catalogued them. (It is their twenty-third entry in her ASBO book of shame—a new record.)

Monday 7
Grandpa and Treena have decided to postpone the wedding until after the baby is born. I asked if this was an indication that they were not going to flout bigamy rules, but Treena says it is because Berkertex can't squeeze her into anything at the moment. She is huge. She claims she is just eating for two. But I don't think babies need entire tins of Celebrations and six-packs of prawn cocktail crisps every day.

Tuesday 8
Rural studies is not as easy as I was led to believe. Mr Cheesmond (scary giant beard with traces of food;

lingering smell of goat) did a surprise quiz on sheep diseases. I had no idea they were so riddled with illness. I hope Mum does not find out, she will ban me from outdoor lessons and remove lamb from her ever-diminishing menu as well. Although I would never have to do games again, which would be a bonus.

Wednesday 9
Rehearsals went well i.e. Davey MacDonald did not get his thing out once, which is just as well as I have to dance within five inches of his exposure area. I think Mr Vaughan is regretting casting Sophie as Blousey though. He has timetabled a load of extra individual rehearsals for her. Obviously she is not measuring up to expectation.

Thursday 10
Mum's anti-binge-drinking letter is in the *Walden Chronicle*. It says:

> As a mother of two, I am astounded that the council is sending out the message that all-day drinking is something to be encouraged. There are already no less than two homeless alcoholics

(aka Barry the Blade and Mrs Simpson)

> marauding our ancient Tudor
> streets, I do not think we want to
> see any more. In any case, the
> pavements are simply not wide
> enough for café tables—have we
> forgotten the catalogue of
> accidents when Gayhomes

(crap hardware shop)

> allowed a perilously wide display
> of mops to overcrowd
> Hill Street.

I wish she would sign her letters anonymously. Thin
Kylie and Cherie (who both have severe Bacardi Breezer
habits) are bound to have something to say.

Friday 11
As predicted, I am, once more, at the receiving end of
post-*Walden Chronicle* wrath. Mark Lambert asked if I
was one of those 'Hamish' people with the bonnets and
clogs and Tracey Hughes said the police were backing
24-hour drinking as their hours were so unpredictable
it was the only way they could fit in a pint before
work.

It is Scarlet's birthday tomorrow. She will be fifteen. I
am going to get her an appropriate card and present to
prove my undying friendship. Sad Ed says she is not

253

having a party. She is going to have a silent gothic mass instead.

- -

Saturday 12

Went into town to get Scarlet's card and present (copy of *Frankenstein* and some fake blood). Am going round there after tea to give them to her.

9 p.m.

Sad Ed lied. Scarlet was having a party. I distinctly saw merriment (upper school goths and Suzy nodding their heads to waily music) through the window. Even Justin was there. Scarlet doesn't even like Justin. I left my present on the doorstep but Jack opened the door to let Gordon and Tony out for a wee at the same time and saw me. He said, 'Shit, are you crying, Riley?' I said, on the contrary, they were tears of joy at not having to listen to such crap music with a bunch of pseudo-vampires. Jack said, 'She doesn't mean it. She loves you really. We all do.' Then he offered to walk me home but I lied and said Dad was waiting for me round the corner. Which meant I had to hover near a Passat until Jack went in.

I walked back via Sad Ed's. As predicted, he was not in but was at Scarlet's joining in the goth celebrations. It is not his fault. He is torn between his friends. And Scarlet is winning because she has an iPod and a vegetarian goth coat.

- -

Sunday 13

Remembrance Sunday

Went to Remembrance Parade with James and Grandpa to 'honour his friends and colleagues who lost their lives in the wars'. I had said I wasn't going (being anti-war is essential in Year Ten) but then Grandpa got all animated about if it wasn't for people like him I would be eating bratwurst and Werther's Originals now (which is rubbish as he eats the latter anyway as a matter of choice and I am not even sure they are German). He is still deluded about his role in the Blitz but I agreed to go none the less. I am honouring innocent men who died heroically trying to protect my freedom and that of weaker nations—not the muppets like Finbarr O'Grady who joined up because they like guns and drinking games.

. . . .

Monday 14

I have my six-monthly appointment with Mrs Wong tomorrow. Mum has scheduled it for four o'clock in anticipation of the blood loss and general carnage. So I don't even get a day at home sipping emergency Lucozade and missing double maths to compensate.

. . . .

Tuesday 15

Cannot speak. Can barely write through the pain. Have had another filling. I do not understand it: I use Colgate, floss, and plaque-revealing tablet things. Maybe Mrs Wong just likes inflicting pain.

Sad Ed came over after tea (Covent Garden soup through a straw) to see if I was still alive. He says that dentists get paid more for carrying out painful and complicated procedures. This is outrageous. Does Tony Blair know of this dental corruption? I am going to take it up with Suzy, as soon as Scarlet and I are on speaking terms.

Wednesday 16

Sophie and Justin were not talking to each other in rehearsals today. As Sad Ed said, 'Something is rotten in the state of Denmark.' (He got this off *True Romance*. He is now hoping to be Christian Slater and specialize in borderline insane acting roles before dying young. I pointed out that Christian Slater was still alive but Sad Ed says, with increasing life expectancy, thirty-six is positively premature.)

Thursday 17

Mr Vaughan has asked Sad Ed to tone down Fat Sam's eye rolling and mental grinning because *Bugsy Malone* is light-hearted comedy, not *Goodfellas*. Sad Ed told him that Christian Slater wasn't in *Goodfellas* and Mr Vaughan said, 'Sorry, I didn't get that. I thought you were being Joe Pesci.' Sad Ed is sulking. He says his weight and slightly diminutive stature (he is only 8 cm taller than me) are hampering his career.

. . . .

Friday 18
Something is definitely rotten in Denmark. I saw Sophie in tears behind the mobile science lab. Mr Vaughan was comforting her. He is very understanding for a teacher. It is because he is only twenty-three and can remember what it is like to be young and in love.

. . . .

Saturday 19
Granny Clegg rang to ask if we were going to Cornwall for Christmas. Mum said we couldn't as Dad is on emergency standby for work (what emergency could this be—a glitch in the Bic biro supply?) Anyway, this is not true. It is because she is paranoid about Hester Trelowarren's battery hens giving us bird flu. Her lie backfired though. Granny Clegg said that they would come to Saffron Walden instead then. Mum did not look happy when she hung up. She has not recovered from the dog visiting rights episode.

. . . .

Sunday 20
James has got an audition for his school nativity tomorrow. He is going to do a scene from *Lord of the Rings*

257

playing both Frodo and Gollum. I offered to give him some tips but he said he didn't need advice from a bit-part player.

* *

Monday 21

Oh my God. My life could be about to change. According to Sad Ed, who heard from Scarlet who heard from Jack, Sophie has chucked Justin Statham. She told him on his lunch break at Goddard's on Saturday. This was a rash move, considering the proximity of the mincing machine. Apparently there is a third party involved. This is excellent news. He will be distraught and get stage fright and I will coax him out of his terror and win his heart at the same time. Hurrah.

* *

Tuesday 22

Saw Justin at the Coke machine at first break. He looked pale and needy. So I pretended to have got the wrong thing out of the machine (i.e. a Double Decker) and said he could have it. But he said he is allergic to raisins and gave it to Jack. Jack said he would swap it for his Twirl but it was all getting too complicated so I gave up and went to watch Fat Kylie menace some new Year Sevens.

* *

Wednesday 23

Rehearsals were fraught with tension. Sophie burst into tears three times and had to be taken to the upper school toilets by Fiona and Pippa for emergency mascara application. Mr Vaughan looked worried. He should have expected it though—all theatrical types are emotional and needy.

Thursday 24

Mum is in a state of panic. 24-hour licensing comes in today. She is convinced the town is going to turn into Amsterdam and that drunken youths will rampage past Woolworth's at 8 a.m., high on a breakfast of Special Brew and cocaine. If only. The only drink-related crime incident to date is when one of the O'Grady's drank ten bottles of cider as a dare and stole a police dog. The police got in trouble as well for having such ineffectual Alsatians. Anyway, it is an excellent law, which will turn dull market towns into continental café societies.

Friday 25

Once again Mum (and me, to some extent) are being forced to eat our ill-chosen words. It turns out that none of Saffron Walden's landlords applied for 24-hour drinking. Mum is claiming partial victory—she says it is her forthright campaigning that dissuaded them from the lunacy of it all. I fear it is more likely their general laziness and unenterprising spirit.

. . . .

Saturday 26

I take it back. There has been some drinking law related hoo-ha—Barry the Blade was arrested at one in the morning for causing a scene outside Abrakebabra. He had purchased late-night lager from Stavros the Greek and was singing 'Push the Button' with his trousers round his ankles. Clearly Stavros is the only forward-thinking businessman in Saffron Walden. It is a shame that his main customer is a renowned psychotic tramp.

. . . .

Sunday 27

First in Advent

Walked past Scarlet's twenty-seven times today. I miss her. There is nothing to do on a Sunday. Plus Sad Ed is at an enforced Aled Jones convention in St Albans. Had to come home though when the dog saw Tony and Gordon on the roof of the Volvo and set off the alarm trying to get them.

. . . .

Monday 28

James has got the lead role in the St Regina's nativity play. According to Reverend Begley, he shows natural

260

talent. This is typical. I am being outshone, theatrically, by an eight year old.

. . . .

Tuesday 29

Oh my God! The third party in the Sophie Jacobs/Justin Statham break-up was Mr Vaughan. Apparently his 'comforting' behind the mobile science lab went a bit further than an arm around the shoulder (a hand inside the Wonderbra, according to Pippa Newbold). Luckily she is already sixteen or he would be joining former Geography teacher Mr Ingham on the sex offenders' register (Leanne Jones triumphs yet again). As it is, he has been banned from directing the school play. Mr Wilmott is putting someone less impressionable in charge (i.e. Mrs Butfield (aka Buttface)—notoriously strict Head of English). Sophie Jacobs is out as well. She is back on the hockey pitch with the lesbians from tomorrow.

. . . .

Wednesday 30

Mrs Butfield is going to recast Blousey. There is an emergency audition on Friday. Hurrah—I am bound to get the role. There is no way Fat Kylie can fit into the costume.

Grandpa and Treena came over for tea. Grandpa looked nervous. It is because Des is being released tomorrow. Treena says they are going to stand their ground and demand to keep the house.

december

Thursday 1

Treena and Grandpa have moved in with us. They are
going to go on the council waiting list for a flat. They
will have a long wait. There are several O'Gradys to
rehouse first. Mum is not speaking to Dad. She says her
house is being turned into a hostel for deviants and wild
animals (Treena brought Christina with her). At least it
will keep Auntie Joyless away. Mum has booked
Christina in at the vet's tomorrow for a thorough bird
flu check-up. Until then it is in quarantine in the garage.
The dog is overjoyed at their arrival. It chased its tail
inanely round the dining room in celebration for over
an hour. I fear it is not loyalty but Treena's crisp habit
that is making it so happy, though. She is now on eight
packets a day.

Friday 2

My audition for Blousey went well. I think Mrs Butfield
was impressed at my word perfect delivery and my
innocent wide-eyed stare (although Sad Ed says it makes
me look like Miss Beadle). Oh, I want the part so much.
I will have to kiss Jack and Sad Ed (Mr Vaughan wrote in
a bit where she sleeps with Fat Sam to get the job to
make it more realistic) but it is small price to pay for
the ultimate prize—snogging Justin at the after-show party.

Christina has been given the all-clear (at a cost of
£57.65). Mr Mercer told Mum that the risk of a domestic

budgie catching bird flu was more than fourteen million to one. But Mum said that was what they say about the lottery and look at the Britchers.

· ·

Saturday 3

Christina has gone missing. It is because Grandpa left the cage open so that she could fly about during *Dick and Dom*. Treena is beside herself. She says it is a sign from God. Mum is more concerned that there will be poo on the soft furnishings. She has covered the three-piece suite with cling film and spare towels.

Plus the dog is ill. It has been retching for hours now to no avail. It has taken over Christina's quarantine spot in the garage until it shows signs of improvement.

· ·

Sunday 4
Second in Advent

The mystery of Christina's disappearance is over. The dog has produced a pile of green-feather-studded sick in the garage. It also brought up a sock and part of a Pringles box. Luckily I removed the evidence before Treena or Mum could find out. It is better that Treena thinks Christina has flown to her freedom on the Peter Purvis Recreation Ground rather than that she was chewed to death by an insane mongrel.

· ·

Monday 5

Today is a milestone in the emancipation of gay and lesbian people across the country. Civil partnerships (aka big, fat gay weddings) are now legal. I think it is lovely. Sad Ed can get married now and I can be his maid of honour. Grandpa Clegg rang up to moan. He says Tony Blair is letting 'deviants like Elton John and that bloke off *Strictly Dance Fever*' run the country. Dad said he didn't know why anyone would bother with getting married if they didn't have to. Mum demanded to know what he meant by that and then we all got sent to our rooms to do our homework (Grandpa and Treena included).

Tuesday 6

Mrs Butfield is going to announce the recasting tomorrow. I am sick with anticipation. Sad Ed says he has put in a good word as well. He is just terrified it will be Fat Kylie. She will crush him, even with his bingo wings.

Wednesday 7

I am Blousey Brown! I knew it all along. Both James and I are theatrical—we are like Jake and Maggie Gyllenhaal or the Fienneses. Thin Kylie is going to take over my role. She and Davey MacDonald are made for each other. They are both perverts.

I got a cheer and a drama club hug. I note that Scarlet

did not join in though. She is annoyed I have a bigger part than her plus I don't have to wear fake facial hair. We have emergency rehearsals tomorrow to re-establish trust (i.e. lots of hugging and falling over). I hope I get paired with Justin.

Thursday 8
I did not get paired with Justin. Instead I had to catch Sad Ed when he fell backwards into my arms. I missed. He is very heavy. He claims it is his bones but it is more likely the layer of fat on top of them. Thank God Mrs Butfield has cut our snogging scene. Ed said she was compromising Mr Vaughan's artistic vision but Mrs Butfield said she didn't think the vision of a drug-smoking paedophile was valid.

Friday 9
Rehearsals were ruined again when Davey and Thin Kylie got done for partial nudity inside the wardrobe department (aka the wardrobe). Mrs Butfield suggested we put in some extra practice in our own time and off school premises where she couldn't be held responsible for our behaviour. Jack said that we should all meet at his tomorrow. Hurrah—I will get to be in the black bedroom with Dandy Dan (which sounds like Cluedo). Admittedly Sad Ed, Scarlet, and Jack will be there but it

is so dark Justin and I are bound to bump up against each other. I will make sure of it.

Saturday 10

Went round Jack's house for rehearsals. Scarlet was out with Suzy and Bob at a sex toy trade fair in Chelmsford. She is obviously avoiding me—no one in their right mind would choose to view a load of dayglo vibrators. Or to go to Chelmsford, for that matter. I asked where Justin was and Jack said he was at Sophie's in a last-ditch attempt to lure her away from Mr Vaughan. He has no chance. Mr Vaughan has a car and can get into Cinderella Rockefeller's.

Then Sad Ed texted me to say he had stayed up late for an *Angel* marathon on Sky and was feeling faint and would be over later when he had eaten several bowls of Crunchy Nut Cornflakes. I bet Christian Slater doesn't ring up Oliver Stone or whoever and say he can't make it to the set because he is watching homoerotic vampire shows and needs to eat cereal to recover.

So it was just me and Jack. Jack pointed out that we had yet to 'crack' the kissing scene and that maybe we should practise a bit so that it is not totally weird when we do it for real next week. He said it wouldn't mean anything, it would just be part of acting, like wearing pubic wigs. I said he was right. It is just tongues and the brain is not involved at all.

So he kissed me. But something weird happened. Because no matter how hard I told my brain not to be involved it just got involved. But, luckily, Suzy walked in with a sex toy that looked like a rabbit and asked if I (gross) or my mum (grosser) wanted to test drive it. So I said I would ask her immediately and ran out before Jack could say anything.

What is going on? Do I like Jack? Does Jack like me? Oh God, it is opening night on Thursday. What if people can tell? What if Justin can tell? He will never love me if he knows I actually kind of like kissing Jack. I will have to do visual projection and pretend Jack is Auntie Joyless. It is the only answer.

Plus now I have Suzy's rabbit-shaped vibrator. I am not going to give it to Mum. She will have Suzy arrested. I am going to give it to the dog. It is the first time I have actually wanted it to destroy something.

9 p.m.
The dog did not like the taste of the sex toy and spat it out during *Casualty*. James is using it to massage his feet. Thank God Mum and Dad are at Clive and Marjory's.

. . . .

Sunday 11
Third in Advent
Treena's baby is due tomorrow. She is now so vast that she cannot climb the stairs and is sleeping on the sofa

with the dog. She is beginning to smell. James suggested to Mum that we could manhandle her into the shower later but Mum did not look thrilled at the thought of viewing Treena's expanded regions. She is going to get Grandpa to sponge her down after *Popworld*.

Monday 12

No baby. I do not blame it staying inside. Our house is not the serene cocoon of whale music and Mozart as recommended by Dr Miriam Stoppard. The dog is in a barking frenzy (it is Natasha Kaplinsky's fault—she sends the dog into a blind panic for some reason) and Treena and Grandpa are arguing about childcare. Grandpa is refusing to learn how to put on a Pampers. He says it is women's work. He is going to be in charge of entertainment. I hope the baby likes Lulu and Gillian McKeith. James asked Treena if she is going to breastfeed (I am not sure if this is out of fear or hope—her breasts are unfeasibly gigantic). She said she night give it a go at home but that no way is she 'flopping her la-las out in Woolies'. I do not blame her. Society still rails against breastfeeding mothers. One of Suzy's Labour friends, Astrid, says she got thrown out of Gray Palmer for breastfeeding her son Felix in the sports support department. Apparently Astrid told Mr Gray that breast was best and he said, 'Not in Saffron Walden, it isn't.'

Tuesday 13

Had my costume fitting. Surely Sophie Jacobs cannot be this thin. Mrs Mathias and her GCSE needlework class are putting in extra darts and an invisible expansion panel. It had better be invisible. It is opening night on Thursday and I do not want to look like Emily Reeve in her homemade pinafores.

When I got home Mum said she had a suspicious phone call from Suzy about a rabbit and did I know anything. I said I had borrowed a copy of *Watership Down* and forgotten to give it back. I then did a Mum-style forensic sweep of the house to locate the vibrator. It is in James's doll collection and is now called Big Bunny. It is overlord of all the toys on account of its ability to vibrate and glow in the dark. I said he could keep it as long as he says he found it in Treena's room and puts one of Will Young's jackets on it.

Wednesday 14

Dress rehearsal was not an unmitigated success. Fat Sam used his splurge gun on Dandy Dan at point blank range and he had to go to Mrs Leech for impact injury. Why does Sad Ed hate Justin so much? Unless it is not hate—it is love. Oh, that is it! He loves Justin! Oh my God—we have the same taste in men—it so totally *Will and Grace*! No wonder he has always told me to stay away from him. Who will win? I predict it will be me. Justin is definitely

272

not gay. He has done it twice (pre Sophie Jacobs), if school rumour is to be trusted.

. . . .

Thursday 15

8 a.m.

It is opening night. I have not slept. This is what Gwyneth Paltrow must feel like every day. Mum, Dad, and James are coming. They are bringing Grandpa and Treena, providing that she is not in labour and that they can roll her off the sofa and into the Passat. They are going to leave BBC1 on for the dog to keep it company.

10 p.m.

It was a triumph. Nearly everyone knew their lines and I did not sing out of tune. The Jack snog was still weird. But I visualized Auntie Joyless, which helped a bit. Although I think Jack wondered why I shuddered at the end of it.

When we got home the dog had had some sort of panic attack and eaten one of the arms off the sofa. Dad checked the TV schedule. Natasha Kaplinsky was doing the news. Mum has added her to the banned list. She has never liked her anyway—it is the choppy hairdo. She thinks all newsreaders should look like Moira Stewart.

. . . .

Friday 16

Tonight's performance was marred only by Dandy Dan firing his splurge gun at Mr Vaughan and Sophie Jacobs who were sat on the third row openly holding hands. It is gross. Mr Wilmott should be stricter. So should Mr Microwave Muffins. I may well write to Tony Blair on Justin's behalf to complain. Also, Mark Lambert climbed on to the stage to join in the final fight scene and knocked out Sad Ed. On the plus side, Ms Hopwood-White says it is the best school production she has seen since the Retards and Criminals did a scarily convincing *One Flew Over the Cuckoo's Nest* two years ago.

Saturday 17

Tonight is our final show. I would be sad but the after-show party could be the beginning of a new era for me. I hope Sad Ed isn't too disappointed.

11 p.m.

A tragedy has occurred. Scarlet has betrayed me in the worst way possible. I cannot bear to write it down. I may well die of sorrow and anger in the night. If I do, and someone finds this, it is all Scarlet's fault.

Oh—and someone tell Mr Wilmott never to use his ruler again. Thin Kylie used it to measure Davey MacDonald's thing in his office after the show.

Sunday 18

Fourth in Advent

I did not die. And I feel revived enough after my Shreddies to write about my ordeal.

Scarlet has snogged Justin. It is unbelievable. It was during 'I Believe In a Thing Called Love' as well, which she knows is my and Justin's song. I was talking to Jack and he said, 'Listen, Riley, I need to tell you something.' But before I could find out what it was I looked over at Goth Corner and there was Scarlet in her vegetarian leather with her tongue in Justin's mouth. Which is what Jack must have been about to tell me. So I burst into tears and then Sad Ed got back from the crisp machine and saw what was going on and threw himself at Justin (a sure sign of gay love) and floored him and Scarlet, then Jack tried to break them up but Sad Ed was too heavy.

Then Scarlet started screaming about how I was deluded and I said, 'At least I'm not a traitor,' and she said, 'At least I don't think oral sex is a biology exam.' (This was unfair—it was in Year Six and I don't have Suzy as a constant source of sex instruction.) So I said, 'At least I don't have a moustache,' (she was still in costume), so she said, 'At least I don't think my second-best friend is gay when he's actually in love with . . . ' but at that point Sad Ed covered her mouth, so Justin hit him and then Mrs Buttface came over and pulled everyone apart (she has superhuman upper body strength) and gave us all detention.

I will never forgive her. (Scarlet I mean, not Mrs

Buttface.) She has crossed an uncrossable line. Sad Ed agrees. He walked me home and held my hand all the way. He understands how I feel. He has been betrayed as well. By Justin and Scarlet. Scarlet clearly does not recognize his innate gayness like me. She has no sixth sense about these things.

8 p.m.
Jack has just rung to check I am OK. He said Scarlet is racked with remorse (not because of me—because she has broken her goth vows and snogged someone who wears Gap). He has invited me to Bob and Suzy's New Year's Eve party (tsunamis and hurricanes allowing). Maybe I will kiss Jack at midnight. That would annoy Justin for sure. Plus it is quite nice, when I am not thinking about Auntie Joyless.

9 p.m.
I have reconsidered and decided I may forgive Scarlet after all. Have done a mental list of possible new best friends and it is limited to Tracey Hughes, Oona Rickets, and Emily Reeve. Obviously there is Sad Ed, my GBF (gay best friend), but I need a girl as well. He gets squeamish about tampons and leg hair.

Monday 19
8 a.m.
It is detention tonight. Maybe it will be like *The*

Breakfast Club with me as Molly Ringwald and Scarlet as the one with dandruff. We will bond as I remove her cloggy goth make-up and turn her into a pale-faced beauty.

6 p.m.
Detention was not like *The Breakfast Club*. There were no wise caretakers to chat to (Lou barely grunts), no one wrote enlightening essays about being a prom queen, a jock, and a basket case and no one smoked drugs when Mrs Buttface was on the loo. I had to sit in between Davey MacDonald and Thin Kylie (in detention over the ruler incident) and write about the life cycle of newts. Scarlet did not speak to anyone, not even Justin. Jack said she is in shock.

Walked home with Sad Ed. I asked him if he was going to Bob and Suzy's party. He said he would if I would. So we have made a pact.

. . . .

Tuesday 20
Davey MacDonald is leaving next term. He got talent spotted on Saturday by someone from the Royal Ballet. They are going to regret it if he insists on showing all those highly strung ballerinas his special needs. Thin Kylie is devastated. She is being comforted by Mrs Leech with a packet of Minstrels.

. . . .

Wednesday 21

First day of winter and last day of school.

Thin Kylie has recovered from her devastation, chucked Davey MacDonald and is back with Mark Lambert. Apparently it was Mrs Leech who told her to do it. They were all over each other during Ms Hopwood-White's all-faith-embracing Festive Assembly.

Scarlet actually said goodbye after school. It is exactly five months to the day since our fight. I hope it is nearly over. Otherwise I will have to borrow one of James's dolls and befriend Emily Reeve next term.

Thursday 22

9 a.m.

My life is reduced to watching *The Brave Little Toaster* with fat Treena and the dog. (Still no sign of the baby. If it is not out by Boxing Day, they are going to induce.) In contrast James has a jam-packed seasonal calendar. He is out looking at the Bishop's Stortford Christmas lights with Mumtaz and is going to a Library reading of *A Christmas Carol* tomorrow, starring Marlon and the least famous McGann.

10 a.m.

I have made a decision. I am going to Scarlet's to forgive her. It is the season of joy and goodwill after all. And even goths celebrate Christmas.

5 p.m.

Hurrah! Scarlet and I are best friends again. I said I forgave her for snogging Justin and she forgave me for letting a chav into my life. I asked her what it was like kissing him and she said she has blocked the incident from her memory, plus she had had an illegal bottle of Diamond White so it was all a bit blurry anyway. She has sworn not to go near him again as a sign of sisterhood and true goth faith. Plus, according to Jack, Sophie found out about the Scarlet snog from Pippa and is thinking of taking him back.

I did not tell her about Jack and the weird kissing thing. She might see it as anti-sisterhood. I asked her who Sad Ed was really in love with and she said it didn't matter as it was clearly never going to happen. She says he is definitely not gay though. She lent him one of Suzy's homosexual instruction videos and he reported no signs of arousal. This is very disappointing news.

Friday 23

Granny and Grandpa Clegg are not coming for Christmas. Mum was so relieved she opened up a box of Elizabeth Shaw mints. Auntie Joyless's Metro has finally broken down irreparably and Dad said he couldn't fetch them as he is on emergency hospital duty for when Treena goes into labour. Granny Clegg said it was a good thing that the Metro was dead as she didn't want to witness the 'child bride' and her illegitimate offspring. She is expecting it to be like Damian in *The Omen*.

Went into town and bought Scarlet emergency Christmas present—black nail varnish and a Marilyn Manson annual. I hope she has got me something. I do not want to be out of pocket present-wise.

Saturday 24

Christmas Eve

Still no sign of the baby. Grandpa is on twenty Benson and Hedges a day to calm his nerves. They have tried hot curry but to no avail. The midwife has told them that sex can bring on contractions but Grandpa says there is no way he is trying it on with Treena when she is that size and that angry.

Went to James's nativity at the church. He was not Joseph, as had been previously suggested. He was Jesus (who, admittedly, is the lead role). He got the part due to his freakish ability to lie still. Plus he was the only one to fit in the manger.

Christmas presents asked for:

- *Jaws* (seminal Spielberg movie and essential viewing for literary types according to Sad Ed)
- *Desperate Housewives* Complete Season One Boxed Set on DVD (*The O.C.* is so over, according to Scarlet. Only Year Eights and Suzy will be watching it next year.)
- An iPod. How can I possibly be part of the iPod generation with an outsize CD Walkman that has had

280

'The Best of Gareth Gates' stuck inside it (James borrowed it to block out the sound of Grandpa and Treena last summer).

I predict I will get none of the above. As usual.

Sunday 25

Christmas Day

I was right. Christmas presents received:

- Grandpa and Treena—*Finding Nemo*. It was the only fish-related film Ducatti Mick had.
- Mum and Dad—David Attenborough boxed set. *Desperate Housewives* has, unsurprisingly, made it on to Mum's banned list (too many reasons to list).
- James—a signed photo of Davina McCall (possibly forged, as obtained in the playground off someone called 'Mad Harry' for £1.80 and a broken tamagotchi).
- Granny and Grandpa Clegg—a £2 record token and a metre-long Toblerone (sell-by date last October, Trago Mills price ticket £1.99).
- Sad Ed—a diary. It has the Ophelia picture on the cover. Only not chewed or covered in caramel.
- Scarlet (thank God)—a black T-shirt. She is trying to lure me into the ways of the goth. She has no hope. My mum will never let me go out looking like a corpse.

Ate non-traditional bird-free Christmas lunch (i.e. roast ham)—turkey, goose, and duck are banned until Waitrose is declared flu free, and beef has not been seen

281

in the house since Mad Cow disease. Then watched *Top of the Pops* with Grandpa and Treena. A song about a JCB digger is Number One. This is yet another reminder of how middle-class and thus rubbish my life is. Why can't Dad drive a digger? No one would write a song about driving around in their dad's air-conditioned Passat.

4 p.m.
Oh my God—Treena has gone into labour. She was trying to make it to the upstairs toilet (downstairs loo blocked following hot curry episode) and the effort brought it on. Dad has taken her and Grandpa to Addenbrookes. He is annoyed because it has interfered with the revealing of the new Doctor Who. Mum is annoyed because Treena's waters broke all over the cream carpet. She has stayed behind to Cillit Bang the landing.

10 p.m.
Feel sick. It is Sad Ed's fault. He came over to commiserate about presents (he got a Scalextric and a Junior Ready Steady Cook Ice Cream Maker) so I opened up the Toblerone to cheer him up and before I knew it we had eaten it all. I should not be doing things like this at my age, I am fourteen for God's sake.

11 p.m.
Have just had weird thought: maybe Valentine card was from Sad Ed, not Justin.

11.15 p.m.

No, definitely not. Sad Ed is just trying to cheer me up with pictures of tragic death. Obviously.

Monday 26

Boxing Day

Bank Holiday (UK)

I have a new uncle. He was born at five minutes to midnight after three epidurals, two tanks of gas and air, and something that looked like a sink plunger, according to Grandpa. They have called him Jesus. Really. Mum said she thought it was illegal but James said that, *au contraire*, it is a common name on the continent and that it is only the British who think it is odd. So Mum sent him to his room to write thank you letters. Auntie Joyless is going to go mad. She is always banging on about the second coming of Jesus and now here one is in Saffron Walden, dressed in a Bart Simpson babygro, with a geriatric father and a crisp-addicted mother. I expect it is not what she had hoped for.

5 p.m.

Jesus Harvey Nichols-Riley is home. He is asleep in a Moses basket on the sideboard. Grandpa is a changed man and is hovering with a Pampers awaiting any signs of activity in that area. He says it is down to witnessing the wonder of birth and seeing Jesus coming out of

Treena's undercarriage into the world. It is gross. Treena said he wouldn't be so joyous if he had thirty-seven stitches in his minky. She is not breastfeeding. I think Mum is relieved. She is in charge of sterilizing—it is a dream job for her.

6 p.m.
Cherie and Terry have been over to wet the baby's head. Cherie and Treena discussed the horrors of birth while Terry drank several of the miniature whiskies I gave to Dad. I asked how Kylie was. Cherie said she was down Barry Island testing out Mark Lambert's new minibike. She is a chav cliché.

Tuesday 27
Bank Holiday (UK)
The joy of new life is wearing thin already. Jesus woke up seven times in the night. Grandpa has taken two of Treena's painkillers. All the getting up and down for feeds and nappies is playing havoc with his lumbago. Only Treena is looking rested. She slept through it all and is on the sofa watching James Bond and eating leftover ham.

Rang Scarlet. She got *Desperate Housewives* Complete Season One boxed set so I will be able to immerse myself in postmodern suburban tragedy at her house, thank God.

Wednesday 28

Jesus was up six times last night. If this goes on I will have to move into the Aled Jones shrine at Sad Ed's. Mum has rung the council to demand Grandpa and Treena are placed at the top of the list for a new flat, but the housing department (i.e. someone called Mr Lemon) is on annual leave until January. She asked what would happen if Uttlesford District were suddenly swamped with refugees in dire housing need in the next week. The receptionist told her it was inadvisable to use words like swamped, but that she had the authority to put them up at the Travelodge at Junction 8 on the M11.

Thursday 29

The dog has taken a dislike to Jesus. It growls at the Moses basket menacingly and has eaten two babygros and a box of formula. James said it is jealousy and we should pamper the dog with presents. He has already given it a double packet of Penguins and a box of All Bran.

7 p.m.

The dog has had an 'incident' in the hallway. It could not get out of the house fast enough to reach the garden. Mum has added All Bran and other high-fibre products as dog food to her banned list.

Friday 30

Scarlet came over so we could plan our outfits for tomorrow night. She is wearing a black corset (one of Suzy's eighties cast-offs) and combat trousers to show both sides of her goth femininity. I am wearing my black T-shirt and the perilous miniskirt and Converse boots because it is the only outfit that does not have Cow and Gate sick (Jesus and dog) on it.

- -

Saturday 31

New Year's Eve

6 p.m.

New Year resolutions checklist:

1. Drink coffee. Not achieved—unless you count Mum's decaffeinated Nescafé and a coffee flavoured Walnut Whip.
2. Get boyfriend. Briefly achieved. Though admittedly not Justin Statham, as anticipated.
3. Buy flattering clothes. Achieved—not counting the flea-infested jumper episode.
4. Train dog. Not achieved. Today it ate Jesus's cradle cap shampoo and foamed all over the carpet. Mum called the emergency vet thinking it had rabies but then it threw up the bottle cap thus averting a national crisis.
5. Get period. Achieved. Am no longer freak of nature being outdone by overdeveloped eleven year olds.

Although it is not all it is cracked up to be quite frankly. It is just messy and expensive. I may well write to Gordon Brown demanding that he provide sanitary products on the NHS. Or maybe I will get Suzy to do it. She has more sway in those circles.

6. Befriend more tragic and interesting people. Not sure if Thin Kylie counts. Although the shoplifting episode was certainly tragic. And Sad Ed being possibly gay for several months was a step in the right direction.

7. Visit Paris. Achieved. Although not the literary and romantic experience promised by *Sex and the City* etc. and clouded by memories of hideous coupling of Mark Lambert and Fat Kylie.

The doorbell has just gone. It will be Sad Ed to go to the party. I cannot wait. I may decide to kiss Jack after all. It is certainly a literary sort of thing to do i.e. snog your best friend's brother. The romantic poets were all at it. I will ask Sad Ed's advice. He is bound to agree. He likes Jack.

6.15 p.m.
Oh my God. It was not Sad Ed. It was Will! He is on the sofa with Grandpa admiring Jesus. He made Fiona drive him all the way here from Fulham. Granny Clegg gave him directions so it is a wonder he arrived at all. He says he made a mistake and he cannot live without me. Mum panicked and invited Fiona in for some Duchy Originals but she had to get back to London—she and Rory are

going to an organic beer and Twiglets party at David Cameron's eco-house in Notting Hill. Oh God, what am I going to do? I cannot take him to Bob and Suzy's. She would go mental if she knew I had snogged a Tory. Plus he does not look like I remember him at all i.e. the nice one out of Busted. He has been struck down with acne. It is vile. Even the dog shied away from him.

The doorbell has just gone again. I hope it is Fiona to take Will away. Or Sad Ed to take me away.

6.35 p.m.
Aaagh. It was Thin Kylie. She is traumatized because one of the traveller girls from the fair is pregnant and claims it is Mark's. (Her exact words were, 'That retard has got some f**kin' gyppo up the duff and Fat Kylie's in Ireland, innit.') She is on the sofa with Will and the dog watching Grandpa feed Jesus and drinking the last of the miniature whiskies. Kylie said she might 'get one of them' this year. Mum said, 'What, a dog?' and she said 'No, a baby, duh.'

Why does nothing good happen to me? All I wanted to do was get a boyfriend and be more vintage and I have ended up with an illegitimate uncle called Jesus, an alcoholic shag-happy chav as a friend, and an ex-boyfriend who has turned into the before bit of a Clearasil commercial.

The doorbell has gone again. Please God let it be Sad Ed.

6.45 p.m.

It is Boaz. I cannot take it any more. I am going out the window, *Dawson's Creek* style. Hopefully they will all be gone by next year (i.e. when I get back from Scarlet's) and life will be back to normal.

6.50 p.m.

I hope Sad Ed left the ladder up.

Joanna Nadin was born in Northampton and moved to Saffron Walden in Essex when she was three. She did well at school (being a terrible swot) and then went to Hull University to study Drama. Three years of pretending to be a toaster and pretending to like Fellini films put her off the theatre for life. She moved to London to study for an MA in Political Communications and after a few years as an autocue girl and a radio newsreader got a job with the Labour Party as a campaigns writer and Special Adviser. She now lives in Bath with her daughter and is a freelance government speech writer and TV scriptwriter. She has written five books for younger readers, several of which have been shortlisted for awards. *My So-Called Life* is her first book for Oxford University Press.